THE CONVICTION
OF HOPE

JANEEN ANN O'CONNELL

PREFACE

This is a work of fiction. However, most of the characters are real, they existed: their births, marriages, criminal convictions, travels, and deaths, are real.

ACKNOWLEDGMENTS

This book would not have been possible without the help of the critiquing group Wordsmiths of Melton. Chapters were submitted for critiquing and feedback was both constructive and supportive.

Huge thanks to Denise Wood – Alpha Reader extraordinaire - always happy to provide the feedback necessary to improve the quality of the work.

Debra Hammer and Janine Thomas – wonderful beta readers not afraid to let me know what they thought.

Nicole Hilder, Family History Librarian at the City of Melton Library and Learning Hub, generous with her time and encouragement.

Dr Robyn Hunter for her support and advice.

This book is dedicated to my children:
Kellie, Beau, Skye
and my grandchildren:
Thomas, Audrey, Paige, Lily and Aysha

Descendant Chart – James Bryan Cullen – First Fleet – *Scarborough*, 1788 and Elizabeth Bartlett – *Marquis Cornwallis*, 1796

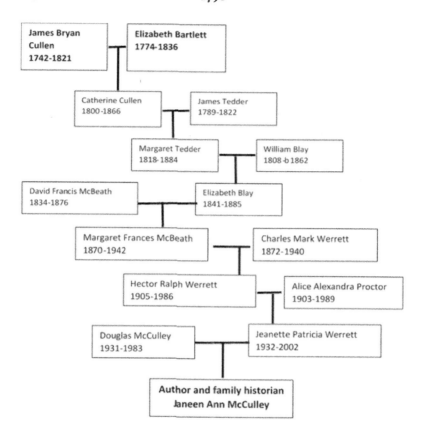

1

"Case number 449 JAMES BRYAN CULLIEN (sic) indicted
for feloniously stealing, on the 12th day of March last, one
pair of thickset breeches, value 1s. 6d. two cloth coats, value
18s. one fustian waistcoat, value 2s 6d. one pair of leather
boots, value 6s. one pair of leather breeches, value 10s. 6d. one
pair of cotton stockings, value 2s. one linen shirt, value 1s. one
pair of leather shoes, value 5s. one pair of worsted stockings,
value 3s. and three muslin neckcloths, value 3s. the property
of John Crandell; two cotton caps, value 2s. one woollen cloth,
value 1s. one silk and cotton waistcoat, value 12s. three cotton
waistcoats, value 19s. three pair of worsted stockings, value
7s. three pair of worsted stockings, value 6s. one pair of
breeches, value 17s. one linen shirt, value 6s. two handker-
chiefs, value 1s. one pair of silver knee buckles, value 5s. one
pair of leather shoes, value 5s. and one silk handkerchief,
value 2s. the property of John Shingler." [1]

At forty-three, James Bryan Cullen was past his prime. Walking into the court room at the Old Bailey, determined to appear frail and elicit pity from the judge, he played on the features of age. Dropping his shoulders he stooped, and limped into the dock. Shoved by a guard, he fabricated a coughing fit.

Cullen fidgeted while the bailiff read the charges against him. Difficult to get his defence to sound plausible, in his own head he knew convincing the judge would be difficult, especially since John Crandell, someone he thought he could trust, squealed like a pig.

Directed by the judge to ask his questions of the witnesses, Cullen rested his hands on the edge of the dock, pretending he needed its support to stay upright, dropping his head lower and lower.

'Are you well?' the judge asked

Cullen nodded.

'Get on with your questions then.'

Cullen wiped his mouth with the back of his hand.

He knew the gavel would bang on the bench with the word "guilty" echoing in its wake. But the sentence of seven years to Africa had him clinging to the edge of the dock, willing his hands to stop shaking.

The bowels of the prison hulk *Ceres* reeked of desperation, fear and hopelessness. Cullen could see his breath against the darkness of the walls. Breathing faster because of his own dread, he looked around to see if others in the group were doing the same. Smoke-like puffs of breath left the mouths of all the men dumped below deck on the rotting old ship. The scurrying of rats as feet shifted on the cold floor added to the terror.

They were to sleep on straw on the floor. No pillow, no mattress. Cullen held the blanket they had given him up to the light, wondering how much warmth a threadbare piece of wool would offer. One privy bucket in the corner to service all the men crammed into a space designed for half as many, was already overflowing. Cullen made his way to the side of the old ship trying to steal a breath of air from the outside: the stench of vomit, urine and shit seeped into his skin.

At the ringing of the morning bell the convicts, backs aching from lying on the floor and necks cramping from the draughts creeping through the cracks in the hulk's sides, struggled to their feet. The hatch opened and a drizzling rain filtered in through the morning light. A wave of anticipation moved through the men. It rolled along carrying with it the hope of a reprieve from the suffocating odours that cloaked them. The mood lightened. But when guards did not appear to unlock the door to the cage, the hope flittered away through the open hatch.

Cullen turned to the boy standing next to him, a young boy, still with the faint look of hope in his eyes. 'Do you know what's to happen?'

'No more than you. Haven't even had a chance to say goodbye to me ma.'

'I've got no one to worry about saying goodbye to, the woman I called my wife turned on me at the trial to save her own skin. Can't blame her I suppose. Name's James Cullen.'

'John Carney. You goin' to Africa?'

'That's what the judge said. Sentenced to Africa for seven years. No one has come back from Africa, you know. I'm thinking I might have to do myself in before I get there.'

'I don't want to die in Africa, either.'

'How old are you, John?'

'Born in 1769 in winter. Don't know. Can you work it out?'

The rage that bubbled up in his gut as Cullen worked out the boy was sixteen and had been in custody since he was thir-

3

teen, threatened to lurch out of his mouth like vomit. Taking control of himself Cullen told the boy he was sixteen. 'I'm old enough to be your father, lad. I don't' have a son of my own, so if you like, I'll do my best to look out for you.'

The hatch opened every day for five days; it was the only way to judge the passing of time. On the fifth morning Cullen cast a wary eye at John Carney. The lad looked sickly on the first day, today his pale face was dotted with red blotches, his eyes sunk into their sockets, and he stooped like an old man when standing and walking.

'You're not looking fit, John.'

Carney shrugged. 'I've been sickly most of my life. The time spent in the gaol in London sucked any of the health I had left, right out of me. There's nothing I can draw on. And without my Ma's remedies and cooked suppers, I don't know how long I'll last. Ma brought food to me in prison when she could. I don't see myself making it to Africa.'

Lumbering down the steps from the upper deck a guard yelled orders 'Get ye up and get ye stuff. Ye goin' to the hulk *Censor*, while ye wait to go off on ye merry way to Africa.'

The thirty men held below for five days climbed the ladder to clean air. Cullen moved his hand to shield his eyes from the crisp light of a London winter.

'Put ye hand down, ye no good convict,' yelled a guard with a cudgel. The weapon landed on Cullen's arm with a thump that vibrated up towards his head.

His first response, to hit the guard in the face, made its way down his arm almost to his already clenched fist. Hearing orders from beyond the line of prisoners ahead of him, he unclenched his fist and took deep breaths to calm himself.

4

Hitting the guard would mean lashes with the cat-o'-nine-tails, and probably a death sentence. Forcing his fingers to relax, Cullen shuffled with the other prisoners to the edge of the hulk's deck.

The transfer from the *Ceres* to the *Censor,* both anchored on the Thames at Woolwich took the best part of the day. Cullen supported John Carney when he could. Owned privately and under contract to the British Government, the prison hulk *Censor,* like the *Ceres* was a floating dungeon. As his eyes became used to the dark below deck, despair settled in the pit of Cullen's stomach; there were twice as many men on this vessel, confined to the same amount of space.

'Listen up you vagabonds,' a voice roared from the top of the steps which led to fresh air and freedom. 'On *Ceres* we gave you a linen shirt, brown jacket and breeches. You'll get a new set each year. We don't know how long you'll be here. You are all going to West Africa and when you need to know, we'll tell you. While you're on the prison hulk *Censor* you'll work. This time of year, winter, you'll work seven hours a day. In summer it'll be ten to twelve hours. You'll work on either river cleaning projects, stone-collecting, timber cutting or embankment and dockyard work. If you prove you can't be trusted, you will do this work in chains and be fettered twenty-four hours a day. Best make sure you eat the food you're given; you'll need your strength to work. You'll get two pints of ale four days a week.'

Finished with his instructions, the man attached to the voice disappeared into fresh air and freedom. The hatch closed behind him. While their eyes readjusted to the darkness Cullen listened. He could hear some men sobbing, some dry retching, some mumbling to themselves and others speaking quietly to those around them.

Moving to stand next to Cullen, John Carney asked him what was to happen to them.

'I don't know, lad. All we can do is work where and when we're told, keep out of their way, and not get flogged or fettered.'

'I've already been in custody since July 1782, James. I got seven years in Africa instead of being hanged. It's already been three years.'

Putting his arm around John, Cullen pulled him in close. 'I know lad, it's not right. We'll keep looking for the opportunity to do ourselves in rather than go to Africa.'

2

Last week of February, 1787

Looking at John Carney's sunken eyes, grey skin and lank, thinning hair, James Cullen wiped a tear from his eye. The lad's health had deteriorated in the last two years. 'Even though I've done most of his work and given him food from my plate, he looks like he's dying.'

'What's the matter James?'

'Nothing. Musta got something in my eye today, it's a bit sore.'

Carney's next comment was stifled before it left his mouth; one of the hulk's senior guards stood outside the locked cell door calling for attention.

'We are goin' to be rid of ye all come tomorrow. Ye'll be put on wagons in the mornin' and taken to Portsmouth. Ye'll be shackled all the way. Don't want none of ye thinkin' ye can make a run for it. And just in case ye haven't got wind of it yet, the government has closed the West Africa post. Ye'll going to New South Wales.'

The men closest to the steps heard the guard cackle as he climbed back to his authorised fresh air.

When Cullen looked at John's face, he imagined looking in a mirror. Horror, fear, terror, were etched on the boy's brow and around the corners of his mouth. 'It will be all right, John. At least we're not going to Africa.'

'I've never heard of the place. What did he say?' Carney's voice croaked with the dryness brought about by dread.

'He said New South Wales. All I know is Captain James Cook claimed some place ten or so years ago at the arse end of the earth for the King and called it New South Wales. It's a long way.'

Cullen sat on the wooden floor that used to be covered with straw and now leached the lost lives of men and boys condemned to the other side of the world. 'At least it's not Africa,' he said again.

'Get up.' The guard's irritating screech pierced the quiet. 'Line up near the steps.'

Cullen was awake. Worrying about what lay ahead and how John would cope nagged at his mind and kept him tossing most of the night. The threads of fear worked their way behind his eyes and pulsed there in a relenting throb of pain.

'Make sure you got all your belongings. You ain't comin' back.'

Cullen got to his knees and pushed himself to a standing position. Lying on the floor for two years had made his back and knees creak like the old ship. He pushed John in front and shuffled behind him into the line.

John, remembering a trinket of his mother's made to collect it from his sleeping space on the floor. Noticing the guard raise his cudgel, Cullen pulled the lad back.

'I have to get something of my Ma's,' Carney complained.

'You can't lad. He was about to thrash you. I don't want you dying on this shit heap. You must keep it in your heart.'

Waiting for them at the top of the steps were rusted fetters and chains. When Cullen's were fitted, he couldn't stand up straight. Bent over like an old man with a hunch back he crawled and slid down the rope ladder that led to the tenders. The skin peeled off his palms as he tried to steady himself on the rungs. Above and below him, unable to coordinate their hands and feet and manage the chains, men fell into the inky water of the Thames. No attempt was made to rescue them. Cullen could hear John Carney, below him on the ladder, praying with each step that if he slipped, God would take him quickly.

Too tired, wet and terrified to complain, the prisoners slumped on their hands and knees on the floor of the small boats as their keepers took them ashore.

Thirty open horse-drawn wagons lined up in a convoy on the other side of the dock area. The rattling of chains and shackles as the broken souls made their way across the dock-side area to their assigned transport echoed through the silence of the early morning.

Climbing into their assigned wagon, Carney collapsed on the floor. A cudgel meant for the young lad thumped on Cullen's back as he bent to help John to his feet. Gasping for air, Cullen ignored the pain in his back, put his arms under Carney's and lifted him to his seat. Sitting on the bench next to his young friend, Cullen leaned forward, head in his hands, trying to control the pain.

Once the provisions for the three-day journey to Portsmouth were loaded, guards chained the prisoners in place. From a position high above, they watched over their consignment of felons.[1]

Pulled by four horses, the wagons lurched forward, leaving Woolwich in a cloud of dust. A sadness not felt since his father died, closed Cullen's throat and made it impossible to swallow. Looking back towards London, the grey pall that hung over the city and the port, mirrored in the colour of the Thames, seeped into his soul. 'One way or another I won't be coming back.'

With ice clinging to its edges, the wind penetrated the threadbare rags hanging on Cullen's shrinking frame. Looking along the line of fellow prisoners, he knew he wasn't suffering alone. Sitting next to him, Carney shivered so violently Cullen thought his teeth would fall out. 'Here, lad. Move in close. That's all I can offer you.' Cullen wanted to put his arm around John to warm him, but with his own arms chained, closeness and an encouraging word would have to do.

As darkness and misery descended on the first day of travel the prisoners were unchained from the floor of the wagon and led, still shackled feet and wrists, into a large barn next to a highway inn.

Glancing over his shoulder at the welcoming, warm light coming through the windows of the inn, Cullen could hear the conversations and laughter of normal travellers. He wondered if he would ever again be a man free to travel where and when it suited him.

Dropping to his knees, Cullen managed to turn and sit on the floor with his legs slightly bent in front of him. The chains didn't allow his legs to straighten and his knees throbbed from being in the same position all day. The skin around his wrists was broken and rubbing raw from the pressure of the cuffs.

'At least the straw is clean,' John said while positioning himself next to Cullen.

Cullen lay on his side on the straw, knees pounding, back aching, head throbbing.

. . .

'Three days,' thought Cullen watching the ships anchored at Portsmouth come into view. 'It feels like three hundred.' His eye travelled along the line of the other twenty-nine men shackled to the floor of the wagon. Ignoring John Carney who sat next to him, Cullen took in each man's bearing and colour. To a man their faces were grey, their mouths flopped open trying to get air into their folded lungs and their wrists were red raw and bruised. 'We have lost all hope.'

Although no force was required to remove the felons from the wagons onto the dock at Portsmouth, incorrigible, power hungry guards raised cudgels to strike the backs of those who moved too slowly, groaned, or complained. The prisoners lined up along the dock with their backs to the sea.

Walking up and down the line of felons, his hands clasped behind his back, the marine in charge spat his commands at the men.

'I am Captain John Marshall, the master of *Scarborough*. You will be loaded on to my ship for the journey to New South Wales. However, there has been a delay in the fitting of the cells below deck so we will house you on *HMS Gorgon* until *Scarborough* is ready. The remaining chains will be removed once you are on board *HMS Gorgon*.'

Finished his lecture, Marshall strode away from his charges.

The quarter deck of *HMS Gorgon* was scrubbed and organised. Cullen leaned against Carney to get his attention, 'It's not a prison hulk.' Allowing his heart a glimmer of hope that their time on this ship might be bearable, he managed a smile.

The *Gorgon's* captain stood in front of the convicts, back straight, uniform impeccable, a threatening look in his eyes. While he rambled on about the rules and punishments, about cleanliness and responsibility, Cullen watched the spittle fly from his mouth whenever he used "sh", which was often. He noticed the right side of the captain's lip curl up when he looked at the men and he put a kerchief over his mouth when one coughed or sneezed.

When the speech finished, Cullen understood the ship was much more important to its captain, than the souls who would call it home for the next few months. The only comment Cullen remembered was that guards would remove the chains and fetters.

The time spent on *HMS Gorgon* gave the men an opportunity to regain some dignity and to physically recover from the depravations of the hulks. Down on his aching knees on the floor, Cullen scrubbed the boards of the sleeping quarters; even though getting up and down was an effort, the resulting cleanliness had improved the health of the inmates. The food although bland, was filling and most prisoners had gained a little weight. John Carney had colour in his face, fullness to his hair, and purpose in his walk. The stay on *HMS Gorgon* healed bodies, some souls, and a few minds. But Cullen's mind filled with the dread of the unknown.

3

"The challenges that Phillip faced seemed to grow in inverse proportion to time remaining before departure. With there being little more he could do with regard to planning and preparation, he was looking more towards the voyage, and the need to ensure that as many people as possible survived what could well be a very arduous, nine-month passage. On 12 March 1788 after the Navy Board had advised him that no changes could be made to the victualling of Royal Marines personnel during the voyage, he wrote to Lord Sydney in protest. Every one of the eleven ships would be severely crowded, and that combined with a poor diet, would almost certainly lead to a considerably greater loss of life. In particular, the very limited supply of flour was most concerning...

In a bid to minimise the chance of disease impacting on all members of the flotilla, Phillip requested of Lord Sydney that any new prisoners be "washed and cloathed" before leaving jails or hulks. He confirmed that some fevers had broken out among the convicts already aboard Lady Penryn.

As was too often the case, Phillip's request was ignored.

Over the months leading up to the fleet's departure, there had been considerable speculation in the press regarding what the death toll among the convicts would be during such a long passage. Their accommodation, diet and the weather were expected to deliver a heavy toll. Some predicted an inordinate number of fatalities – 80 per cent – while others were more conservative.

Determined to minimise the inevitable death toll on the voyage, Phillip had implemented the best possible diet for everyone, convicts included. The evidence of this is in the fact that the weekly food allocation for sailors and marines was only one-third more than that for the male convicts, while the women and children received a slightly different menu. Whenever the fleet was in port, every effort would be made to supply fresh food." [1]

12th May 1787

Cullen sat up with a jolt, banging his head on the bunk above. 'Shit,' he yelled before lying back down. Rubbing his head he lay on the bunk sorting through the questions running riot in his mind.

Was he pleased the nightmare of existing in squalor on prison hulks was over? 'Yes.'

Was he glad to be underway on the voyage he'd been threatened with for two years? 'Not so sure.'

Was he sad to be leaving England? 'No.'

Was he apprehensive about the journey and what lay ahead? 'Certainly.'

Going through the new set of *Scarborough* rules, Cullen

rejoiced a little: they'd be able to go on to the upper deck for fresh air, exercise and to wash themselves and their clothes.

Rumours about Captain Arthur Phillip, leader of the Fleet, who neither Cullen nor John Carney had seen, painted a picture of a fair man who tried to secure just conditions for his charges.

'When do you think Captain Phillip will tell them to let us out of here?' Carney asked Cullen while the Fleet made its way towards the southern end of the English Channel.

Cullen, feeling the effects of the sea sickness afflicting most on board, yelled at the lad, 'I don't know. How would I know? Leave me alone and go cry to someone else. I'm sick of you.'

His outburst over, Cullen picked up the pillow and put it over his face and ears to soften the sound of the vomit symphony that raged around him.

With no one else to talk to, John Carney lay on his bunk moving his body with the rolling of the ship, listening to the waves crash against the side of the vessel, and to other men vomiting and cursing. Two, who seemed unaffected by the seasickness that wracked most of the convicts confined below deck, huddled together in a corner, whispering. Carney moved closer to the end of his cot, trying to block out all other sounds, so he could listen in.

'We's goin' ta havta wait till they let us up on deck for air and washin then we'll push the marines overboard and rev up these other worthless convicts ta help take o'er the rest of the ship.'

'That sounds like a good plan.'

Carney slid back down and put his head on his pillow. His heart raced so quickly he put his hand on his chest to slow it down and stop it from jumping right out of his skin. These men were talking of mutiny and young John Carney needed to tell someone. Hesitant to approach James Cullen for fear of being yelled at again, John steeled himself for an opportunity to tell a marine – not a sailor – a marine. A marine would report to the captain.

'Tell me exactly what you heard,' Captain Marshall ordered. 'Don't leave anything out.'

Standing on the other side of the captain's desk, hands clasped in front of him so he could limit their shaking, Carney told Marshall exactly what he heard the two men say.

'Thank you, lad,' the captain said. 'I'll have this matter reported to the commander of the fleet, Captain Arthur Phillip. I will remember your courage and honesty on this voyage. Marine, take him back to his quarters.'

Not to raise suspicion as to why Carney had been taken away by the marine, he was shoved heavily in the back when making his way down the steps to the convicts' quarters. Coughing from the severity of the attack, Carney squatted on the floor waiting to regain his breath.

'What happened, lad?' Cullen asked rushing to John's aid.

'Nothing. Leave me alone. I'm sick of you,' Carney lashed out.

Ignoring the lad's outburst Cullen helped John to his feet and over to his bunk. 'I deserved that. I'm sorry for abusing you the other day.'

Carney pushed Cullen's arms away from him and rolled onto his side with his back to his protector. Laying on the bunk Carney fretted about his decision to tell the captain about those planning to take over the *Scarborough*. If the other convicts found out it was him, they would kill him.

. . .

A marine opened the hatch, moved onto the steps that led into the convicts' quarters and called them to attention. Outlining the events about to unfold, he said 'You will be allowed on deck to exercise and wash yourselves. The weather has calmed. If you cause my marines or any of the sailors any grief, you will be flogged.'

John Carney watched as the convicts made their way to the steps. He positioned himself in the group's middle, avoiding attention. As the two conspirators, who were ten men in front of him, made their way onto the deck, each was grabbed by a marine and dragged away. Carney let out the breath he had been holding.

"This was Phillip's first chance to be seen exerting his full authority over the expedition, and he had no hesitation in doing so. Once aboard the Sirius, both prisoners were tied hand and foot, probably to the mainmast, and flogged two-dozen times by the bosun's mate, with no mercy being shown. They were then transferred to Prince of Wales, where they would remain...

With the emergence of this plot to mutiny, it would have been understandable if Phillip had ordered a more strict watch over all the convicts throughout the fleet. Instead, he appears to have applied a degree of reverse psychology, by easing one of the regulations regarding prisoner security to ensure they were treated more humanely... 'where they judged it proper, they were at liberty to release the convicts from the fetters in which they had been hitherto confined...'"[2]

They haven't come back.' Carney said to Cullen when the bells rang next morning for the start of another day sailing on an endless ocean.

'Who hasn't come back?'

'The two men the marines grabbed yesterday and dragged away. What do you think has happened, James?'

Fighting the urge to raise his voice at Carney and remind the boy that he didn't have a crystal ball, Cullen said, 'I don't know, lad. They've obviously done something bad because they were sent over to see Arthur Phillip on *Sirius*. We'll find out soon enough.'

July 1787

Cullen watched helplessly as John Carney thrashed around on the floor. Frothing at the mouth Carney's eyes rolled back in his head and he bit his tongue. Cullen lay down next to the boy and held him close, watching the contortions of his face, struggling to contain the thrashing, he readied himself for the lad's death.

Carney was not the only one fitting in the oven below deck on the *Scarborough*. Using a bench seat to bang on the hatch a convict got the attention of a marine and the hatch opened. Looking up into the face of someone who had the opportunity to breathe air that wasn't tainted with spittle and vomit, he asked for the ship's surgeon. 'Men are fitting and are unconscious.'

'There's nothing the surgeon can do. We are in the doldrums on the Equator and here we will stay until the wind picks up.' The hatch closed.

Cullen sat with legs out straight, nursing John Carney's head in his lap. The lad had stopped fitting but was unconscious. Unable to wake him, Cullen ladled water from the rations, over Carney's brow; he didn't stir. Looking around their prison, it shocked him to see dozens of men lying on the floor, some fitting, some prone. He hoped none of them died in this furnace; the bodies would soon smell.

There was no respite. With no ventilation between decks the transportees languished in their hell until the fleet crossed the Equator.

14th July 1787

Carney's tongue hurt when he tried to eat the salted pork Cullen offered him. Preferring to drink the ale and leave the food until later, Carney gulped his fill and sat back on the bunk. Cullen's frown and piercing gaze made the lad uncomfortable. 'What are you looking at?'

Smiling at the question, Cullen said 'I'm glad you're all right now, lad.'

On deck as the *Scarborough* made her way into the Southern Hemisphere, the prisoners watched as King Neptune came aboard for the *crossing the line ceremony*. Entertaining crew and convicts alike, King Neptune and his queen led the celebration as *Scarborough* moved from one hemisphere to the other.

'How do they even know we are moving into another hemisphere?' John asked.

'They use a sexton. As King Neptune initiated the sailors who hadn't crossed the Equator before, seasoned sailors knew where we were. And we'll have a whole new sky overhead. But we won't see it until we are landed.' Cullen explained.

Celebrating the crossing of the Equator gave John Carney a boost, and he made his way to his bunk, pulling the piece of salted pork Cullen had offered him for dinner from under his pillow. Grinning, he sat on the floor, inviting Cullen to sit next to him. With his friend as company, Carney scoffed the meat as if he hadn't eaten for days, not offering any to the man who had held him close and kept him safe while he thrashed around from the effects of the heat.

Life on *Scarborough* returned to normal for the first two weeks after the crossing. While the fleet headed for Rio de Janeiro the prisoners exercised on the deck, cleaned the cell they slept, ate, vomited and toileted in, washed themselves and weather permitting, their clothes. This routine added a lift to Carney and Cullen enjoyed seeing the young man look more his age. The mood on the prison deck improved with the sailing conditions.

5th August 1787

With unfathomable darkness surrounding the flotilla it sailed into the port of Rio de Janeiro at eight-thirty on the evening of 5 August 1787. Those on deck the next morning were greeted with a wide, sparkling bay hugged by rugged mountains and carpets of green.

Like caged lions, the convicts paced up and down on the prison decks of the ships in the fleet, grumbling at the unfairness of being restricted to the vessels while the alluring beauty of the landscape, and city of Rio lay beyond reach. Cullen understood the rationale of keeping he and his fellow prisoners on board; there weren't enough guards to keep them under control on shore. Confining them to the floating prisons was the only way to manage the numbers. He gazed longingly at the port, his legs twitching with the desire to walk on a surface that didn't move.

'James, James, look,' Carney squealed, bringing Cullen out of his daydream. Turning in the direction Carney pointed,

Cullen noticed small boats being manned by natives, pulling in close so they could throw oranges on board.

The convicts and sailors on deck scrambled to collect the oranges as they hit the boards. Cullen knew they were oranges because he'd seen them in the house of the Lord he worked for. He had never eaten one, but he'd watched while those higher up the social scale did.

'What are they throwing at us?' Carney asked, watching Cullen and the others racing each other to collect the little orange coloured balls.

'They are oranges, lad. Grab as many as you can, they are good to eat, so I hear.'

With arms full, the two men clambered down the steps to their bunks, both hiding their haul under their mattresses, spreading them out so the mattress still lay flat.

Smiling at Cullen, John Carney held an orange up to his mouth and took a bite. Spitting and coughing he spewed the orange peel onto his bunk. Laughing until his eyes watered and his sides hurt, Cullen slapped the lad on the back and told him to clean up the mess. 'Then I'll show you how the eating is done.'

While in Rio, Phillip charged the masters of the ships in the fleet with buying supplies for their vessel. Cullen and his fellow convicts loaded the foods into storage in the galley. Carney asked questions about yams, watermelons, bananas, guavas, pineapples, and mangoes. Cullen salivated at the smell of the mangoes and pineapples. He thought about taking the risk of smuggling a mango into his shirt, but shivered at the thought of the flogging if they caught him.

4th September 1787

Ordered below deck, and the hatch closed behind them, the convicts muttered to each other in speculation about the reason for their confinement. As the familiar movement of the sailing ship rocked beneath them, cheers erupted below deck; they were headed to Cape Town. One third of their journey was now complete.

'I don't think I can take anymore,' John Carney murmured to James Cullen. Both men, along with most of their fellow prisoners, lay on their bunks, confined by the wretchedness of sea sickness. The storm that raged around them was so intense the hatches were battened down to prevent the violent waves cascading water into every available gap.

Cullen's head spun with each contraction of his stomach. The stench and the unbreathable air meant the spinning intensified as the gasps for relief increased.

14th September 1787

'It's stopped,' Cullen whispered to Carney. 'The storm, it's over, the waves aren't crashing over the ship. The hatch is open.'

Dragging themselves from their bunks the convicts encumbered with sea sickness scrambled to get to fresh air. Cullen stood aside to let Carney go first. The lad's face was the colour of mustard, his hair reminded Cullen of a drawing he had seen once of the witch in Macbeth, his hands shook, and his breath reeked like a corpse. Feeling his own hair and rolling his tongue around in his mouth, James Cullen imagined he didn't look or smell much better.

The weather was mild enough for the prisoners to wash themselves and their clothes. Fresh clothing stored with the food stuffs was distributed to the men. Teams collected the washed clothes and headed for the bowsprit end to hang them to dry. As soon as Cullen heard the marine yell that prisoners could stay on deck, he grabbed Carney by the arm and led him to a bench in the sun. 'Sit here, John, you need the sunshine to warm your bones.'

"After thirty days of what had, so far, been a mostly wet, wild and miserable passage across the South Atlantic, everyone in the fleet, from the commodore [Phillip] to the lowliest convict, was relieved to know that they were closing on Cape Town."[3]

13th October 1787

Cullen remembered seeing a painting on the wall in the big house on the estate where he'd worked. It was of a harbour that reflected the blue of the cloudless sky, and then gently swept up to yellow beaches. Beyond the beach, mountains bearing no scars from the interference of man, loomed menacingly. A valley appeared to wander between two contradictory mountains – one had a flat top that could be lost in the clouds - and the other pointed to heaven. The artist had been to Cape Town and with permission to stand on the deck of *Scarborough*, looking across the water, Cullen didn't think the painting had done the place justice.

Cullen's legs wobbled, they hadn't walked on solid ground for nine months and he felt the urge to put one foot in front of the other on a surface that stayed firm under him. The surface he could see, tempting him from just beyond reach, was where he wanted to stand.

'Same rules apply here as in Rio de Janeiro and Tenerife,' bellowed a marine at the prisoners balancing on the deck. 'The Commodore has ordered that marines, sailors, marines wives and children are the only passengers permitted to leave the ships. As long as you behave you can be on deck during daylight. Choose not to behave, and you'll be locked in the cells below.'

Cullen looked down at his legs and shook his head, 'Must wait even longer.'

Apart from not leaving the ship. Cullen and Carney spent a pleasant time in Cape Town. They were bathed in spring sunshine during the day while they worked cleaning, washing and repairing items from their below deck prison, slept soundly on bunks that rocked gently on the swell of the bay, and ate better than they had since being taken into custody.

"While the convicts were not permitted to leave the ships, Phillip insisted that they have the best diet possible, to ensure optimal health over the final stage of the journey. Their daily allowance included 1½ pounds of soft bread, 1 pound of beef or mutton, plus a generous serving of fresh vegetables."[4]

10th November, 1787

With his clothes and bedding clean, Cullen lay on his bunk thinking about the things he missed most about his previous life. Before his trial he would have said Eleanor Welch, the woman who lived with him as his common-law wife. Now, it was something to read. He'd always enjoyed reading books and plays and when the lord of the estate finished with newspapers, Cullen scavenged them from the pile in the kitchen. A book would help him feel like a man instead of a worthless piece of rubbish cast to the other side of the world.

'How much further is it 'til we get to New South Wales, James?' Carney interrupted Cullen's thoughts.

'The sailors were talking about 6,000 nautical miles and that we are two thirds there. But they seemed worried about it. I heard one say nearly all of it was across treacherous, freezing cold ocean. We've been through some impressive storms though, and we're still here.'

'It's taking so long. My body is about ready to give up.'

Cullen wanted to disagree with John, to tell him he looked strong and would easily survive the last part of the journey, but the lad's appearance confirmed his own estimation of his health. Although they'd eaten well since Rio and while they were at Cape Town, the fresh air, sunshine and better food hadn't made much difference to John Carney. His face still had a tinge of yellow, you could see the purple under the skin on his hands and the skin on his neck and arms was dry, red and peeling.

'You will be fine, John. You're looking much better since Rio,' Cullen lied. 'I'll protect you from doing any of the physical work and keep you warm and dry when we hit bad weather.'

Smiling at James Cullen, Carney patted his friend on the arm, thanked him and made his way to his bunk, curling up in a foetal position he rocked back and forth with the movement of the ship.

4
***

"With the entire squadron having arrived safely, this endeavour could, without question, go down in maritime history as one of the great voyages of all time. Eleven vessels carrying some 1400 people had crossed more than 17,000 nautical miles of ocean, much of that distance through hostile and little-known waters. The duration of the passage was 252 days, and while there had been loss of life, the death toll... could be considered extraordinarily low for the era...The deaths included thirty-six male convicts, four female convicts, five children of convicts, one marine, one wife of a marine and one marine's child. In short, Arthur Phillip had every reason to feel supremely proud of what he had achieved."[1]

19th January 1788

'The hatches will stay open to let in air, but none of you vagabonds will get on the steps or even attempt to make your way to the upper deck. You do, and you'll walk on this new land in chains.' The marine's gravelly voice echoed through the prison.

Cullen winked at Carney, 'We've arrived lad.'

Allowed on deck for a few minutes to look at the shore they wouldn't walk on, Cullen again felt his legs wobble and twitch. 'My legs want to walk on firm ground again John,' he said, looking at Carney whose skin still had a yellow tinge.

'I'm not going to ask when that will be, James. One of the others yelled at a marine demanding to know when we are getting off, and he got a swipe across the face with a closed fist. Knocked him out. The marine shackled him.'

'I'm telling my legs we can wait a bit longer.'

'There's natives on the shore, James. You can see them waving lances at us. Do you think we'll be safe?'

Cullen had hoped with John surviving the ten-month journey he would be less like a jack-in-the-box waiting to pop, and more prepared to take on the new world. Now that sailing treacherous waters was no longer a problem, John appeared to focus on other things he couldn't control, like the natives.

'After what we've been through, I think Arthur Phillip will take care of the natives,' Cullen said as he settled on his bunk for the night.

'Be ready for sailing on the morrow,' a marine shouted as the cell doors closed on the men. 'Fleet is moving to another harbour, the Commodore said this one's no good.'

26th January 1788

Cicadas chirping, a cacophony of different bird sounds and the spectacular scenery of the newly named Sydney Cove, greeted the convicts on *Scarborough* as they gathered on the deck to see and hear their new home.

Anxious to curtail his impatience, Cullen clenched his fists and tightened his jaw while he watched Governor Phillip and a contingent of marines and convicts walk on the shores of the new land. 'How long are they going to leave us here, watching them?' Cullen muttered to Carney.

'I don't think it will be long, James. Phillip will want us off the ships to get to work soon. Can you see the Union Jack flying near the edges of the trees?'

'Yes, I see it. Makes me crave land under my feet even more. I'm afraid my legs will take off without my permission and get me flogged.'

27th January 1788

'Carney, Cullen,' a marine yelled through the darkness of the below deck prison. 'Get your arses to the cell door so I can see where you are.'

Leaning in close to James Cullen's ear, Carney said, 'It's not even light outside. What do they want with us?'

'Let's just do as he says, then find out.' Cullen sounded more confident than the pit of his stomach indicated. Trying to stop his hands from shaking while he pulled his ragged breeches on, Cullen smoothed his hair, wiped the sleep out of his eyes, and patted Carney on the back.

Standing at the cell door as instructed, both swallowed hard as the marine put the key in the lock. 'Collect any belongings you have, you got 30 seconds.' Looking back at the bunk, Cullen couldn't see anything worthy of the effort. On deck, the two of you. Hurry up about it.'

As the cell door banged shut behind them, the two men climbed the steps to the upper deck of the *Scarborough*. James Cullen took in the biggest breath he had for a few days. The fresh air filled his lungs with life and his heart with hope.

'Look at the sunrise, John. It's magnificent. I've seen nothing as amazing. No sunrise in England ever looked like this.' The sun rose above the horizon, spreading its bright orange and yellow hues out like wings. 'Listen to the birds.'

'You haven't got time to stand and watch the sunrise and listen to birds, convict,' the marine spat in Cullen's face, 'Over to the side, you're getting on the cutter and going ashore. Governor Phillip wants convicts he can trust to get to work. Seems you two fit that description.'

Cullen struggled to keep the grin from spreading across his face, but Carney let his face break into the first smile he had shown since his arrest. Settling into the cutter without chains attached to their feet or wrists, the two men, along with three other prisoners they didn't know, headed to the shores of Sydney Cove.

'When you get out, support each other until you get to the shoreline. Your head will be spinning. You've been on the water for a long time, you'll need to get your land legs,' a marine instructed the men. Holding on to each other for support, Cullen and Carney wobbled from the shallow water to the sand.

'My legs are finally getting their wish,' Cullen told Carney. 'But I think it'll be some time before they can carry me anywhere.'

'Don't sit down,' ordered the marine. 'Stand with your feet apart, facing away from the water. When you feel confident, take small steps. Walk up and down the sand until your legs stop wobbling.'

James Cullen and John Carney obeyed the instructions and by the time the sun had moved from the horizon to an angle that beat down on them, they walked without feeling sick, or falling over.

Before being given axes and instructions about which trees were to be cleared, James Bryan Cullen and John Carney sat with about forty other prisoners on the beach, eating dried beef and biscuits.

'This food must have come from *Sirius*,' Cullen lent in to tell Carney, 'it's better quality than we got.'

Chewing noisily, Carney nodded at Cullen, a grin peeking through his hard working jaw.

'Listen up,' a marine ordered the men. 'Just because you are considered trustworthy, doesn't mean the rules don't apply. Wander off, disobey instructions, slack off your work, you'll be in chains, and put back in a cell on one of the ships sitting out there in the harbour. Got it?'

The group of recently fed prisoners nodded in compliance. Cullen wondered if they were as happy as he to be off the ship, standing on dry land, and with something useful to do.

Set to work clearing trees along the marked boundary it didn't take long for John Carney to struggle for breath.

Like a protective mother bear of her cub, Cullen ushered Carney into a break in the trees. 'Stay there, son, I'll cover for you. Rest and drink some water.' Glaring at the prisoners either side of him Cullen challenged them to keep quiet about Carney.

A break for dinner was a welcome reprieve from the physical labour required to fell trees. Sitting on the sand under the shade of trees yet to be cut down, the prisoners were provided with ale, bread, and fish caught and cooked a few days before.

Cullen put his head back, closed his eyes, and felt the sea breeze float across his face. The smells that accompanied the breeze were a collection of random things he hadn't noticed earlier: the sea had the distinct aroma he had become used to on the voyage, but the trees and the undergrowth smelled like nothing he had experienced. He'd noticed the leaves on the trees had the effect of clearing his head and making breathing in the heat easier, but the ground under the trees had a heavier, dense odour.

'Back to work,' bellowed a marine, bringing Cullen back to the present. 'Clearing as much as you can today, means you won't have to go back to the ships after tomorrow. You'll have room to put up some tents.'

Looking at the ships bobbing up and down on the swell in the harbour, Cullen had no longing to be back on board.

5th February 1788

John Carney struggled to keep up with the group of prisoners selected to build the storehouse to hold the provisions brought ashore from the transports. Still assigned to felling trees, Cullen kept glancing over to his young friend concerned his strength wasn't up to those around him. Working in this guarded environment it wasn't possible for James to cover for the lad.

With the storehouse completed, all prisoners on shore were tasked with removing the provisions from *Supply's* boats and packing them in the makeshift building. Picking up a bag of wheat and throwing it on his shoulder, Cullen felt something move down his arm onto his back.

'There's a rat,' yelled one of the others.

A range of thoughts raced through Cullen's mind like fallen leaves in autumn being blown around in the wind. 'If I drop the bag it will split, and the wheat will spill, and I'll be flogged. If I keep still the rat might start gnawing on me. If I spin around holding the bag, I'll likely fall over, and the wheat will burst out of the bag onto the ground.'

Quickly weighing up his options, Cullen stood still while the men around him waved their arms and yelled until the rodent scurried away into the bush.

There were more uninvited travellers revealed with the unloading of other goods.

· · ·

Two weeks after arrival, Cullen saw Carney doubled over and struggling to pick up the tools required to work. While he'd been busy, Cullen hadn't noticed that there were several men with the same appearance as his friend. The principal surgeon had ordered a tent to use as a hospital soon after landing, and Cullen carried Carney all the way to the western shore [The Rocks] to accommodate him in the tent. Sitting by the lad's cot, he overhead the surgeon talking to Governor Phillip about how pitiful the patients looked and there was nothing available to offer comfort.

'Everyone was healthy on the voyage,' Phillip lamented 'what has happened now?'

'There's no more fresh fruit and vegetables, Governor,' the surgeon answered. 'A lot of the prisoners and the free, have scurvy. And the men are shitting too close to the sleeping quarters. Dysentery is spreading.'

James Cullen wasn't one to pray often, but as he sat next to his young friend, he prayed for a speedy recovery for John Carney.

Aware of the dire circumstances surrounding the shortage of food, Cullen stood with the other prisoners, marines and sailors while Governor Phillip told them about their weekly rations.

'7lb of flour, 7lb of pork or beef, 3 pints of peas, 6oz of butter and ½ lb of rice.[2]. Be a good idea to supplement your diet with fish, and we'll trade with the natives for food. Better still, try to grow your own food.'

Phillip stood for a few minutes after speaking and Cullen thought he looked as if he wanted to say something else, but he turned and left.

'There's talk he's going to send some folks to a place called Norfolk Island,' Abraham Hands, another convict from *Scarborough* said to Cullen.

'Why?'

'There's not enough food here to go around. Stuff's not growing, and we'll all end up with the scurvy or dead.'

'Well I won't be leaving young Carney,' Cullen said, 'they better not pick me without John.'

'Somehow I don't think they'll care about you or Carney, James. Best we can hope is that after all this time to get here, we survive.'

5

"Unless it were at the meal Hours or at Night he was imme-diately sent to work, his back like Bullocks Liver and most likely his shoes full of Blood, and not permitted to go to the Hospital until next morning when his back would be washed by the Doctor's Mate and a little Hog's Lard spread on with a piece of Tow, and so off to work...and it often happened that the same man would be flogged the following day for Neglect of Work." [1]

May 1788

James Bryan Cullen wasn't selected as part of the first group of convicts and marines to go to Norfolk Island in March 1788. Neither was John Carney. Carney hadn't left the hospital tent. James visited him at the end of work each day, getting him out of bed for a little exercise, washing his face and hands, and helping him eat.

'You're looking better, John,' Cullen lied. He realised he'd lied a lot to the boy over the last two years.

'I don't think that's the case, James. The dysentery seems to have passed, but now they say I have scurvy and another disease I brought with me from England. But they don't' know what that is. I'm going to die here, James, on this God forsaken part of the world. I'm going to die in this place, a long way from my home.'

'You are not going to die,' Cullen scolded. 'I won't allow it. You are going to get better, and we are going to earn our freedom and build a life.' Cullen wiped a tear before it had time to trickle down his sunburned cheek.

The injustice meted out to John Carney made Cullen's head ache and kept him awake at night. The lad had been in custody six years, he'd spent one third of his life in the deplorable conditions provided by the English Government. Cullen prayed for this young man more than he prayed for anything else. As each new day dawned on this new land, and Cullen watched the sunrise, his neck ached, his stomach churned, and his head thumped until he could visit his friend.

'They're not the trees we are supposed to be felling,' Cullen yelled at the sergeant overseer. 'They're marked for shingles; we are felling trees to build the barracks. Didn't you listen to the instructions?' As quickly as the words had spurted from his mouth, Cullen knew there would be consequences.

With his fellow convicts staring, mouths agape at his eruption, Cullen watched the sergeant send a guard to the Governor's tent. He waited while two marines, each with a sword at their belt, and one with shackles clenched in his fist, made their way to the sergeant. Steadfast, James Cullen waited while the sergeant pointed him out to the marines. The only thought going through his mind, 'Who will look after John Carney?'

'Drop the axe, convict,' the marine holding the shackles ordered.

Cullen lay the axe on the ground with the butt facing his

feet. Standing straight, he didn't wait for them to tell him to put his hands in front, instead offering them to the marine for the shackles. Shoved in the back by one marine, and pulled along with the shackles like a dog by the other, they pushed and dragged Cullen to Governor Phillip's tent.

Captain Collins, not Governor Phillip, sat on a chair with a large desk separating him from the likes of Cullen. 'You've been insolent to Sergeant Thomas Smith and are hereby charged with using improper words.[2] Twenty-five lashes at sunrise tomorrow. Lock him up.'

Even though he walked obligingly with his gaolers, they pushed and shoved him into the prison tent. The shackles were left on. The cots running along the edges of the tent had been fashioned from the bunks in the transport ships. No other facilities were available. With no chairs, Cullen moved to a vacant cot, and unable to use his hands, plonked down heavily on the low-lying timber frame. Lifting his feet and swinging them onto the bed, he put his head down, his hands on his chest, and closed his eyes. 'Twenty-five lashes. At least he didn't say with the cat. Oh Lord, please don't let them whip me with the cat.'

Knowing he wouldn't get any sleep, Cullen opened his eyes and stared at the flapping roof of the makeshift prison. He was still staring at the roof when the rising sun pierced the flimsy fabric of the tent. He hadn't made any attempt to talk to any of the other ten prisoners in the tent, nor had he eaten the food that was put on the floor before dark the day before. He lay, watching the sun's rays creep through the tiny holes in the tent's roof.

'Cullen, James Bryan Cullen,' the marine shouted.

James willed his legs to go over the side of the cot and twisted his body to sit on the edge. 'I'm here, sir,' Cullen said, making his legs push his body upright. The two marines who had collected him from his work the day before, took position on either side and led Cullen to a line of trees at the edge of the settlement. If he had been less worried about Carney, he would have laughed at the irony, 'This is the same area I worked in yesterday.'

The shackles removed from his wrists; Cullen was ordered to take off his shirt.

'Lieutenant Clark says clothes are too hard to come by, don't want to be ruining this,' one of the marines scoffed at him.

As his hands were tied together at the back of one of the smaller trees, Cullen closed his eyes and begged God to keep him alive so he could look after John Carney.

Standing with his forehead against the tree and his hands immobile around its trunk, Cullen suffered the first two blows in silence. The convict charged with issuing the punishment didn't know Cullen, but through fear of being flogged himself, picked up the whip and struck the sunburned skin on Cullen's back. The third strike had a groan escape. He was silent for the fourth and subsequent strikes. It was an unspoken rule in camp that convicts made no sound when whipped, beaten, or given any other punishment.

The blood was dripping into his shoes when they untied his hands. What he thought were tears trickling down his face, was blood from his forehead banging on the tree trunk with every blow. The convict who flogged him threw a bucket of cold water over Cullen's back. He fell to his knees.

'Get up,' came a roar in his ear. 'Get up and get to work felling the trees you were told to fell.'

The marine's spittle sprayed on the side of Cullen's face. Using the tree to drag himself upright, Cullen shuffled to the edge of the clearing where Sergeant Smith waited.

'Get your axe and get to work. A flogging isn't an excuse not to do your share. Don't do your share, and you'll get flogged again. Plenty more where you came from.' Smith moved away, watching as Cullen struggled to bend down and pick up the axe. He kept watching while Cullen swung the axe behind his shoulders and sunk the cutting edge into the base of a tree. Turning to harass another convict, Smith didn't see the tears pour from Cullen's eyes and run down his cheeks onto his bare chest.

Making sure Smith had lost interest and moved on to another group of convicts, Abraham Hands and Richard Morgan approached James Cullen.

'We'll cover for you today, James,' Morgan said. 'Swing the axe if you notice Smith or any other marines coming this way. Abraham and I will fell your trees as well as ours.'

'Thank you,' Cullen whispered. 'But you will be flogged too if you are caught.'

The day was the longest in James Cullen's life. At the call for dinner, Abraham and Richard helped him to the area set aside in the camp for convict meals. Yesterday the area was under the shade of a huge tree. Today the tree was gone, and they sat in the blazing midday sun. Abraham helped James put on his shirt.

'Keep the flies off, James. And keep the sun from burning you more.'

Cullen nodded a thank you.

Holding his breath didn't ease the pain, but apart from curling up in a ball on the ground and risking another beating, Cullen didn't know what else to do. His back had stopped bleeding, the blood wasn't running into his shoes anymore. But it burned as if a blacksmith's branding iron that never lost its heat, was put on his skin. The burning mingled with the throbbing pain. He drank the water offered by Abraham but couldn't muster the strength to eat.

'I'll get a bucket of sea water for your back,' Richard Morgan said. 'We'll pour it on you through your shirt. It's too painful to take the shirt on and off is it not?'

Cullen nodded in agreement.

Dinner finished, his two friends helped him off the log they sat on to eat and supported him back to the task of tree-felling.

Leaning on the tree he was supposed to fell, for support, Cullen grimaced while Richard Morgan pulled the neck of his shirt back and poured sea water on his wounds. Gasping while the saltwater found its way into the raw flesh, Cullen struggled to stay conscious.

'Thank you, Richard,' he said as his friend finished. 'I have another favour to ask of you. I don't want young John Carney to see what's happened to me. Can you visit him in the hospital tent this evening?'

'Yes, James. I'll visit your young friend and see if he needs anything.'

June 1788

In the four weeks since the flogging Cullen, with the help of his friends, had kept up the illusion of working. The skin on his back was tightening around the whip marks and although the pain had eased, the burning hadn't. Standing as straight as the taught skin would allow, he went to visit John Carney who still occupied a cot in the hospital tent. He'd been twice before but the effort to pretend all was well used up too much energy. Energy he needed to work.

The last time Cullen saw John he was sitting in a chair, reading a book one of the marine's wives had lent him. Cullen didn't remember the name of the book. This visit saw John lying prostrate on his cot, his breathing shallow, his skin as white as the nightshirt he wore and his scalp peeking through clumps of matted hair. Cullen froze, his feet refused to move. Carney was waiting for God to take him.

Frantic for an explanation and a reassuring word, Cullen's feet took him towards the surgeon who was fussing over blood, spattered on his shirt.

'Excuse me, sir,' Cullen said, forcing himself to be polite and calm, making the rage and despair stay trampled in his gut, 'what is wrong with young John Carney? He looks as if he is dying.'

'He is dying. He has the scurvy and dysentery that we can't rid him of. I don't think he will see out the day. Friend of yours?'

'Yes, he is like a son to me. We have been together for three years. He's only a boy.'

'There's no explanation about why some are taken and not others,' the surgeon comforted. 'We've looked after him as best we can. You should say goodbye while he knows you're here.'

3rd June 1788

James Bryan Cullen, his friends, the surgeon, and the marine's wife who'd helped look after John Carney, stood over the newly dug grave that held the body of the nineteen-year-old. The settlement's Chaplain, Richard Johnson's words, said by rote were over quickly. Dropping to his knees, head in his hands, Cullen sobbed for the lad sentenced to death at thirteen. He grieved for the boy who'd spent six years living in squalor at the mercy of an indifferent English government. A trusting soul who hoped one day to be free to return home.

6

SIRIUS again remained in Port Jackson until the 7th March,
1790 when she left on her last voyage which was to Norfolk
Island to land marines, convicts and stores.

The island was reached on March 13, unloading at Cascade
Bay took place on the 13th and 14th of March after which the
passengers walked across the island to the settlement at
Sydney Bay. Heavy weather then kept the SIRIUS at sea for
four days, but when it improved on the 18th, Captain Hunter
lay off Sydney Bay on the south side of Norfolk to land the
provisions.

As the boats were loading from her, the SIRIUS drifted too
far into the bay to get out again and was wrecked on a reef
near the settlement. By a hawser with a traveller on it, all
were saved through the surf, along with much of stores and
provisions but the SIRIUS was a total wreck.[1]

"On 13 March 1790, she arrived at Norfolk Island, with the
SUPPLY, to transfer a group of Marines and convicts. Here,
on 19 March 1790, her life came to an end when the wind

forced her on to the reef, as her Captain, John Hunter, tried to tack out to sea.

The Marines and convicts had been landed before the wreck. After the wreck, the ship`s crew was saved and, in the days and months which followed, the stores and equipment were retrieved. The wreck of the SIRIUS remained visible on the reef for nearly 12 months before a storm forced her from view. The loss of the SIRIUS was a terrible setback for the settlements at Sydney Cove and on Norfolk." [2]

February 1790

Called to muster before work, Cullen strode to the clearing in the centre of the settlement. Government House loomed over the gathering of convict men and women. Mutterings, questioning looks, shuffling feet, and sweat on foreheads, aggravated the anxiety pulsing through the group. With practised obedience, silence fell when Governor Phillip appeared.

'I will not delay you long from your work. If we call your name, you will remain here at the end of muster. If we do not call your name, move off to work.'

There was no explanation. Scenes from the last few days scurried in Cullen's mind like rats over a spilled wheat sack. What had he done wrong?

They called names in what appeared to be a random order. Cullen relaxed when the sheer volume of convicts indicated punishment was unlikely.

'Move closer together so you can hear me,' Captain Hunter roared at the chosen convicts, Cullen among them. 'You are all going to Norfolk Island. Governor Phillip has had you selected as worthy of supporting yourselves in a new colony. If we all stay here, we will starve. Crops aren't growing and livestock is dying or running off into the trees never to be seen again. *HMS*

Sirius and *Supply* will leave next week. Time for you to start a new life. Dismissed.'

They'd sent Richard Morgan to Norfolk Island six months after the fleet arrived in Port Jackson; he left his wife Lizzie behind. Cullen had no concerns about leaving anyone. Since John's death he had kept to himself, worked without correction or punishment and until today, thought he was invisible.

7th March 1790

A wheat sack slung over his shoulder holding his few belongings, Cullen made his way on board *HMS Sirius*. At forty-eight he wondered why, as one of the oldest convicts in Port Jackson, he would be a farmer on an island in the middle of nowhere. He was fit for his age, had avoided scurvy and dysentery and kept out of trouble. He was strong, and since the flogging had worked without complaint. Why would they not keep him in the settlement? It didn't matter where he went, he would never return to England and if the Governor thought he was a farmer, then that's what he would be.

Saturday 13th March 1790

Even though dark rain clouds hung low as *Sirius* and *Supply* encroached on Norfolk Island's treacherous shoreline, the majesty of the lofty trees waving a welcome, and the squawk of sea birds spying on the ships from their position of superiority out of reach of predators, dropped sprinkles of hope into Cullen's heart. The optimism spread through the convicts on board *Sirius*. None had seen anything more spectacular.

With the island tantalizingly close Cullen allowed himself time to think about catching up with his friends Richard Morgan and Abraham Hands. He smiled, picturing Abraham's smile as the two embraced. More subdued but just as friendly, Richard would reach out to shake his hand in welcome.

Marines shouted orders to get below jolting Cullen from his daydream, just as he felt *Sirius* roll from a change in wind direction.

Once again locked in the dark below deck, Cullen felt the ship moving away from Norfolk Island, away from the majestic trees and the cacophony of thousands of birds.

'Are we going back to Port Jackson?' William Thompson, another convict from *Scarborough* asked Cullen.

'Doubt it. Maybe going out to sea to calmer waters. We won't know until they decide to tell us.'

The sound of the anchor being dropped for the second time this day, was the only sign the passengers needed, to know *Sirius* had found another opportunity to land at Norfolk Island.

The hatch opened to let in the grey shadows of the hovering storm clouds. 'Everyone on deck.'

Cullen stood back and waited while the other felons made their way to the upper deck. One of the last to find a place within hearing distance, he listened while the First Mate fought to be heard over the wind as it tried to unwrap the sails tied to the masts.

'This is Cascade Bay. Female convicts and women with children will be offloaded here from *Sirius* and *Supply*, as will the marines. It is a ten minute walk back around to Sydney Bay. The marines will lead the way.'

The male convicts helped the marines organise the evacuation of women and children onto the small boats that bobbed alongside *Sirius* and *Supply*. As the last boat was rowed ashore, navigating its way through the rocks that threatened to splinter it into firewood if it got too close, the grey clouds burst, and their contents poured down on to those standing on shore and those still struggling to get there. Still on deck, rain saturating their clothes and the wind biting their ears and faces, the men waited for orders.

'Captain says we're staying here until the weather settles. No more going ashore today. As you were.'

'First mate seems more concerned about the welfare of his ship than the rest of us,' William Thompson complained.

Nodding in agreement, with nothing more to be done while the wind whipped up the waves, Cullen made his way below deck to ride out the storm and dry off.

15th March 1790

It didn't escape Cullen that he was once again trapped on a ship at the mercy of its captain. Seeing the irony in the restlessness that three days confined to *Sirius* caused when he'd been on ships for three years before landing in New South Wales, Cullen tried to calm himself. Clenching his fists open and shut, moving from one foot to the other, and running his hand through his hair, Cullen struggled with the anxiety.

The weather settled enough for orders to filter through that this day, the rest of the men would go ashore at Cascade Bay.

In pouring rain and biting wind, Cullen and his fellow prisoners climbed down the ladders on the side of *Sirius* and settled into her boats, huddling as the rain penetrated the threadbare clothing they'd worn from Port Jackson.

'There's no-one here,' wailed one man who'd reached the top of the low cliff face.

The wind picked up the response from someone on the sand below and swept it out to sea. Cullen heard '...Sydney Bay, ten minutes.'

Cullen's clothes clung to his frame and dripped water into his worn-out boots. Folding his arms over his chest and shivering with cold, he and the rest of the men walked across the island, following the muddy prints left by the women and children and marines three days earlier. Looking back at *Sirius* wallowing around in the surf, Cullen wished Captain Hunter well.

As the sodden group made its way into the settlement at Sydney Bay, the rain stopped. Shivering with cold and trepidation, the prisoners were ushered around a large fire to warm up and dry off.

Put in tents the first night on the island, Cullen lay on the makeshift bed he fashioned out of branches he'd dragged from under the huge pine trees that towered over the intruders. Exhausted from the events of the last few days, Cullen slept soundly on his bed of pine needles.

19th March 1790

Watching from the cliffs that lined Sydney Bay, Cullen and the other convicts had enough sailing knowledge to realise something was wrong. The wind changed direction and Captain Hunter had *Sirius* turn to sail away from it, but she struck the coral reef and took on water.

All men from the island congregated on the sand and waded into the shallows to help. Some pulled ropes connected to the ship at one end and rocks on the shore at the other, guiding sailors who were abandoning the ship. Some swam into the treacherous water to rescue supplies being thrown overboard.

Cullen, wading into the water up to his waist, to guide floating barrels to shore, marvelled at the skill of Captain Hunter as he tried to navigate his ship away from the rocks that were tearing cavernous holes in her side.

The sea eventually claimed *Sirius*. After five days trying to keep her away from death, Captain Hunter left his ship as she broke up on the rocks. Half of the supplies destined for the Norfolk Island settlement perished with her.

The inhabitants of Norfolk Island, old and new lined the cliffs, watching the tragedy of the *Sirius* unfold. The Commandant of Norfolk Island, Phillip Gidley King, standing apart from the rest of the settlement, removed his hat and held it over his heart.

With the loss of the *Sirius,* the few days after were filled with disbelief and fear. The newcomers used to living on rations and working with grumbling stomachs, fretted that their lot hadn't improved. They worked while hungry and with aching muscles.

'Will we ever get away from this type of life?' Cullen muttered as he and Daniel Daniels a fellow *Scarborough* convict erected tents and stored supplies salvaged from the *Sirius*.

'I hoped to start again here. I brought letters from home. They were in my bag, but no personal belongings have been saved from *Sirius*,' Daniels lamented.

'I had nothing but the clothes given to us in Port Jackson.'

Muster was listed for eight am on Monday 22nd March. Cullen moved with the rest of the Island's population as they were set in position under the Union flagstaff. He watched as the marines and sailors stood on the right and the officers lined up in the centre, below the flag. He moved with his fellow transportees to the left. Cullen noticed Richard Morgan and Abraham Hands and moved to line up with them. Morgan looked particularly fit. He had a glow to his skin and held himself in a relaxed and comfortable way. Hands looked strong and at peace, grinning happily as he hugged Cullen. Cullen's heart skipped a beat of hope.

Major Ross, in full marine regalia, cleared his throat; the shadows from the few clouds hovering in the sky settled on his face. The only sound came from one or two whimpering children. Five hundred and six people who called Norfolk Island home, listened as he asserted his authority. His address started with acknowledging and thanking outgoing Lieutenant Governor Phillip Gidley King.

Cullen looked around in amazement as the three cheers for Gidley King rang louder than the three cheers for King George. Cullen envied Morgan and Hands, it seems they had lived on this island when peace and prosperity prevailed.

A gasp moved across the settlement, like a breeze skipping along the top of a wheat crop as Ross commanded the immediate enforcement of martial law. He lamented that with the loss of *Sirius* not all the supplies had made it ashore and they faced the possibility of starvation.

Cullen felt his shoulders slump. Isn't this why he and the others left Port Jackson: to save that colony from starvation?

Ross continued. 'Every man, woman and child will work to provide shelter and grow food.' He enlightened them with the punishments for breaking martial law. For stealing food to feed oneself, the punishment was death. For stealing food to barter for rum or foodstuffs, the punishment was flogging until the bones showed. Man or woman, the same punishment. He added, raising his voice to a roar, that children would not get off lightly.

The speech reminded Cullen of Governor Phillip's edict on arrival in Port Jackson. The hope that sprinkled in his heart when he first sighted Norfolk Island was melting like the late winter snow on London streets.

'What do we do now?' he asked Abraham Hands. 'There's no barracks.'

Moving close to his friend and putting his hand on his shoulder, Abraham titled his hat back, and said, 'You are almost free here, James. As long as you do as Major Ross said, and grow food for yourself and the settlement, he'll leave you alone. Find yourself a plot of land, build a cabin and find a woman to live with. In the meantime,' he said standing back, 'you can stay with me.'

Accepting the offer of somewhere to stay while he navigated the requirements to get land and build a cabin, Cullen followed Abraham to his cabin like a starving dog who had just been given a morsel of food.

Although simple, Abraham's cabin was comfortable and clean. The timber walls from the sawmill that Richard Morgan managed, kept out the howling winds and driving rain. The windows had shutters that closed to keep insects and weather out and opened to let in sunlight and fresh air. One big, welcoming room had a fire on one side with cooking equipment surrounding it, a handmade timber table and four chairs to the left of the fireplace, and a handmade timber, double bed took up the whole wall on the other side. Cullen stood in the cabin, took in a deep breath, put his head back and said a silent prayer to God thanking Him for sending him to Norfolk Island.

'This is wonderful, Abraham.'

Abraham took off his hat, threw it on the bed, slapped Cullen on the back and told him to sit at the table. 'It is magnificent, James. Those of us sent here to Norfolk Island are blessed. As long as we keep out of trouble and look after ourselves, we are as good as free men. There are other pieces of furniture I want to create when I have the time. But I am well pleased with what I've done so far. I'll set up a bed for you on the floor until you get your own land.'

For the first time since his arrest in 1785, James Bryan Cullen breathed air belonging to those who lived without restraint.

7

July 1791

He stood back, one hand on his hip, the other shading the sun as it tried to find different angles to penetrate his vision. The smile that spread across his face surprised him with its spontaneity. He didn't remember the last time he smiled so widely. He didn't remember the last time he felt this surge of happiness and satisfaction. The little cabin showed off its pride of place on the rise, declaring ownership of the surrounding land. Smoke from the fire he'd set snaked its way out of the chimney, disappearing into the crisp winter air. The hens, with no need to worry about predators, scratched and fossicked in the ground around the front door. This small piece of land, enough to keep himself in food and shelter, was his. Given to him by Major Ross. James Bryan Cullen puffed out his chest, stood with a straight back, and made his way to the garden at the back of the cabin.

'You need a woman to do that work, James,' Abraham shouted from the trees at the back of the block.

Beaming at his friend, Cullen invited him into the cabin for refreshments.

Abraham sat on the armchair Cullen offered and watched as the kettle was placed on the fire to boil. 'Your vegetable garden looks healthy, James. As do your hens.'

Pulling over one of the two kitchen chairs, Cullen sat opposite. 'I really need more land to farm properly. I've only got 25 rods. Not enough for sheep or pigs. But I don't want to get on the wrong side of Major Ross and ask for something he isn't prepared to give.'

'Keep proving yourself on this small parcel of land, James. He will notice. He will offer you a bigger parcel if he thinks you have the skills to manage it.' Abraham sat back in the armchair drinking the tea Cullen had made, and chewed on a hard biscuit. 'These things remind me of the stuff we were fed on the prison hulks. For goodness sake get a woman, James. You can't cook to save yourself.'

The marines arrived at the front door of the cabin to collect Cullen's contributions for the island's commissariat. Reassured his relationship with the authorities was in good stead, even though his convict status remained, Cullen invited the two armed marines into the cottage for something to eat. Offering each one a chair at his small wooden table, Cullen served some fresh bread he'd made that morning, boiled eggs, and dried fish. They washed the meal down with a hot mug of sweet tea.

While helping the marines load the eggs, potatoes, peas and corn he'd packed as his share of the contribution to the settlement, Cullen said, 'If I had more land I could grow more food.'

The older of the two put his hat back on his head and whilst climbing onto the wagon looked over his shoulder, 'I'm sure you could, Cullen. Thanks for the meal and the provisions.'

March 1792

He pulled the bullock to a stop, swivelled around on the wagon seat, shaded his eyes, and took one last look at the little cabin he'd lived in, alone, for the last year. He'd built the cabin, established the vegetable plots, fed himself, kept out of trouble, and contributed to the settlement. Abraham was right, Major Ross had noticed. He wiped the tears from his cheeks; they fell in happiness as much as sadness. Although leaving this cabin, he was heading to a grant of twelve acres at Queenborough Path. He would build a new house, and farm the land a free man. Lieutenant Governor Philip Gidley King had given him his freedom. Cullen would breathe the fresh air of Norfolk Island with renewed vigour. His life was starting over.

Helping Cullen saw timber for the north wall of the new house, William Thompson straightened his back and wiped his brow. 'I'm gettin' used to the heat, James, are you? We've been here just on two years and I thank Governor Phillip every day for choosing me to go on board *Sirius*.'

Cullen nodded in agreement but didn't engage William in further conversation. He wanted to get the house weather tight.

With four walls and a floor completed, Cullen lit a fire outside and put two fish he'd traded for eggs, in a pan on the hot coals. Sitting on the chairs he'd brought from the cabin in Sydney Town, William and he watched the sun disappear beyond the horizon while the fish sizzled.

'Did you ever see the sun set in London, William?'

'No, not once. Wasn't till we were on the ships heading to Botany Bay had I ever seen the sun set. Didn't know it could be so spectacular. But this, here, on Norfolk Island, is more than I could ever have imagined.'

Cullen lent forward and turned the fish to cook the other side. 'I will die here, William. I don't want to go anywhere else. This island is my final destination.'

With intermittent help from William Thompson, Cullen's two-roomed house was finished by Easter. Timber walls, a timber floor, timber slats on the window openings and a roof made from the branches of the Norfolk Island Pine. He'd used stone scavenged from around Sydney Town to build the fireplace and chimney. In time he would add more rooms. Happiness denied to him since his arrest in 1785, seeped into his heart: this belonged to him. Thinking of John Carney and how the lad would probably have had much better health on Norfolk Island, Cullen stood in the doorway of his cabin, looked out over the grass as it waved to the ocean beyond, and promised he would make good for himself and John.

Busy establishing a vegetable garden and ploughing his twelve acres in readiness to plant grain, Cullen enjoyed living on his own. He ventured into Sydney Town when summoned for some announcement or pronouncement, and when he needed supplies. He traded food and services with his neighbours. When Richard Morgan needed help with construction or ploughing, Cullen helped. When William Thompson and Abraham Hands called on him for support, he obliged. They reciprocated, and Richard Morgan, who seemed in favour with the authorities, also got some books for Cullen when ships arrived with supplies from London via Port Jackson.

Cullen spent his days working his farm, helping his neighbours, and experimenting with new ways to use the native pepper he'd found growing near his lot. He spent the evenings sitting by the fire reading old English newspapers and any books Morgan gave him.

September 1794

The marine knocked politely on Cullen's door and waited for it to open. 'Lt Governor King wants to see you in Sydney Town on the morrow afore noon.'

Astounded by the unexpected order, Cullen's mouth opened but no words came out.

'You all right, Mr Cullen?'

Shaking his head, trying to get his brain to function enough to string a few words together, Cullen asked if the marine knew why King wanted to see him.

'You're not in trouble, Mr Cullen. If you were in trouble King would have sent more than just me, and we'd be pickin' you up today.'

Feeling better, Cullen invited the marine inside for a drink and something to eat. Relaxed conversations with marines sometimes revealed unknown events and endeavours going on in the settlement. Pouring tea into the marine's cup and slicing a piece of salted pork from his supply, Cullen asked if King was keeping order in the settlement at Sydney Town.

'There are the incorrigible individuals we have to watch constantly. Even your friend, William Thompson got a few lashes for stealing corn. Seems to have learned his lesson though.'

Cullen heard Thompson had been whipped, but didn't know what he'd done.

'Might be why King wants to see you, Mr Cullen. He's been muttering about needing more constables in the areas where people live away from the main settlement. Wouldn't be surprised at all.'

Thanking Cullen for his hospitality, the marine put his foot in the stirrup and swung his free leg over the back of his horse. Tipping his hat, he bid him farewell.

Cullen watched the marine ride off, worrying about what tomorrow would bring.

Not wanting to waste a trip to Sydney Town, Cullen put some recently harvested grain, eggs, potatoes, and corn onto the wagon, which he would sell to the Stores or barter with other settlers.

'Come in, come in,' King beckoned as Cullen walked into the Lt Governor's office. Offered a seat on one side of a roaring fire which Cullen thought unnecessary seeing as the weather was mild and spring well under way, he took off his jacket before settling on the chair.

'You are wondering why I wanted to see you, so I'll get straight to the point, Cullen. I want you to be Constable for Creswell Bay and West Point Steam District, which takes in your farm. But you'll need to find a wife to run things for times when you are away on official business.' A shrewd leader with excellent negotiation skills, King leaned back in his chair, waiting for a response.

Wiping perspiration from his head because of the heat from the fire, Cullen smiled at King. 'It's warm in here Lt Governor. Are you not too hot?'

'No, I feel the cold. Getting old. You will join me for lunch away from the fire when you have answered me.'

Cullen collected the documents from King that identified him as a Constable and loaded dried fish, dried beef, sugar, salt, tea, and a new supply of reading material onto his wagon. Smirking to himself at the new responsibility which confirmed his status as a free man, and the extra money that would bring, he dared to hum a song he hadn't heard for many years. Lost in his thoughts, King yelling his name, made him jump.

'Cullen, this is Anne Bryant. Her husband died. She needs

somewhere to live, and you need help with the farming. She's leaving with you today. Help her with her things.'

Although a free man, Cullen, like his fellow Norfolk Island citizens was obliged to obey King's instructions.

Cullen knew the woman as Anne Coombes. He smiled politely, tipped his hat, and after loading her belongings on to the wagon with his supplies, he helped her onto the seat where she would sit next to him, for the one-hour journey.

Forced to hold on to her bonnet with both hands, Anne's face screwed up and her eyes half closed against the dust that blew into her face from the wind racing in from the ocean. She didn't answer when Cullen asked if she was all right. He offered no more conversation for the journey and neither did she.

Anne Coombes accepted Cullen's offer of help to get down off the wagon. Her hat blew off her head as she took his hands; it landed next to the bullock. Cullen laughed harder than he had in years as the animal picked up the hat between his teeth and waved it around in the air shaking his head to give the hat more vigour.

'Get it off 'er,' ordered Anne. 'When am I goin' to get the chance to get another.'

Still laughing, Cullen approached the bullock, stroked him on the neck and whispered in his ear; he dropped the hat on the dusty path. Picking it up and giving it a good shake, Cullen handed it back to Anne, grinning.

'It's not funny. I'll have to wash it now.'

Moving to unharness the bullock, Cullen said, 'It won't take long to dry in this wind. I'll unload your things when I have the animal sorted. You're welcome to go inside and look around.'

Banging her hat on her leg, Anne Coombes lifted her skirt, flicked back her hair, squinted against the sun and made her way into James Bryan Cullen's house. She stood in the kitchen taking in its smells and feels. The fire was set in readiness for a cold spring evening. There was a wooden bench under the window with a metal tub suspended halfway through a hole so you could wash dishes without it being too high. A bench on the other wall had two shelves underneath with a piece of netting suspended over the front. She salivated when she saw the dried pork, eggs, sugar, tea, jam, and jars of peppers lined up neatly on the shelves. One large and one small pot, and one large frying pan sat on top of the bench. The kettle hung from its frame over the fire.

Checking her boots were clean, Anne took small steps and headed to the bedroom. The standard of pride in the home carried through to this room. A large double bed placed in the centre of the room was covered with a bright red quilt; two large pillows sat at the top of the bed, leaning against the rough sawn timber bedhead. Woven flax rugs lay on the floor either side of the bed. Anne jumped with fright when Cullen came in.

'You startled me,' she said turning to face him. 'Where did you get the quilt from? England? No-one on Norfolk Island makes quilts that grand.'

Ignoring her question, Cullen put Anne's bags on the floor next to the dresser, and suggested she put her things away and get settled. 'We can get to know each other better over supper.' He closed the door behind him.

While he prepared supper, James Bryan Cullen thought about the two and a half years he'd been on Norfolk Island: he'd built two homes, cleared land, grown food, gained his freedom, and lived alone. Now, because of accommodation shortages, he was obliged to give a home to Anne Coombes. He wondered what sort of companion she would be and if he could rely on her to tend to the house and the vegetable garden.

Anne opened the bedroom door as Cullen put plates and cutlery on the table. He noticed her hair was perfectly in place, and her clothes unruffled. 'Come and sit down, Anne. I've put together some supper.'

Accepting his invitation, Anne Coombes sat at the kitchen table. Cullen laid out freshly baked bread, baked potatoes, corn cobs, peas and a little salted pork. 'That's the end of the pork I'm afraid. I'll trade some grain during the week.' He hoped she was a good cook. He had a limited repertoire.

'Thank you, James. May I call you James?' Without waiting for an answer, she continued 'You keep a clean and organised house, James. Where am I to sleep?'

Taken back by her forthright approach, Cullen took a moment to think. 'Thank you, Anne. I like my environment organised and clean. It's been easy by myself. You'll sleep in the bedroom. I'll set up a bed on the floor in here. I'll build on two more rooms: another bedroom and a parlour, when I can.'

She proved a worthwhile addition to his landholding, Anne did, and she was a good cook. The vegetables flourished under her determined eye, the livestock well fed, and the hens kept laying. It didn't matter where he'd been working, either on the property or as a constable, when he came home for dinner and supper, Anne had a hearty meal waiting for him.

Hanging his hat on the hook just inside the door, and putting his coat next to it, Cullen pulled off his boots and salivated at the smells coming from the kitchen. Commenting on how delicious supper smelled, Cullen washed his hands and sat at the table waiting for Anne to serve the meal.

'I want to talk after supper, James. Before you pick up a book and settle in the parlour.'

Cullen had a feeling he knew what Anne wanted to discuss, and dreaded the conversation. He ate slowly, putting off the inevitable.

As he got up from the table, Anne took him by the hand and led him into the parlour. 'Sit down, James.'

Anne sat opposite in the chair she considered hers and waited while Cullen sat in his. 'I think we should marry. We've been living as husband and wife for a year and a half. I don't want to be the widow Bryant any longer. I want to be the wife of a landowner, the wife of a free man, the wife of a settler.' She clasped her hands on her lap and waited.

This was the conversation Cullen didn't want to have. He didn't love Anne Coombes. She was useful to have in the house and the garden and kept him warm on cold winter nights. But he couldn't bear the thought of spending the rest of his life with her. She farted more than the cattle on the farm, her breath smelled like the privy, her teeth were yellow and broken like the old hags that begged on London streets, and her hair was lank and greasy. But these weren't the reasons he didn't want to marry her; he really didn't like her very much. She was demanding. Her demands included what he should trade in Sydney Town, what he should grow on the farm, and what he should wear when working as a constable. Her latest demand was that she wanted children and he must sleep with her more often.

Looking at the woman across from him Cullen felt a pang of guilt rise through his gullet. He spoke the truth regardless. 'I don't want to marry you, Anne. I'm sorry. I'm too old for children, and I like my life the way it is.' Expecting tears, he readied to go to her side. Instead, she stood up, straightened her dress and spat into his face

'I'm leaving in the morning. You can take me to Sydney Town.'

Watching her flounce into the bedroom he caught sight of the supper dishes and cooking mess he was now obliged to clean up.

8

Dublin, Ireland. February, 1795

He had us in a line in his parlour, the master. It's the room he uses to entertain his fancy friends. Must be killing him to have the likes of us all in there at once. There's six of us. I've been working in this house for a couple of years. I've seen him make his way through the younger girls, grabbing them when he saw fit. Can't imagine how his wife doesn't know what he's up to.

He's looking for his gold watch and a silver pair of buckles. Says he knows one of us lowlife Dublin misfits took them. Franny took them. I watched her do it. She's been working for him for more than ten years in this house, and she's still poor. She sold them to buy medicine for her sick mammy. Franny's mammy must be ancient, cos we think Franny is really old.

He strides along the line of us girls, glaring. I'm not scared of him. I didn't take his stuff, but I wish I had. He stops in front of me, standing so close to my face I can smell his rancid breath. Smells like the rotten meat the cook sometimes uses to make the stew for him. I stand straight and stare back at him. He doesn't like it.

'You stole them.'

The spittle from his rotten mouth sprays onto my face. I lift my hand and wipe it off. This makes him real mad. He yanks hold of my arm and pulls me out of the line. I catch a glimpse of Franny. Her eyes are pleading with me not to say it's her that's guilty.

'You took them, didn't you?' he yells.

This time he's closer to my face. Wants to prove a point, I guess. I wipe my face with the other hand. He moves his arm behind himself, brings it forward quick as, and slaps my face so hard I fall on the floor. Franny screams. I stay on the floor on my hands and knees. My head is spinning. He grabs my hair and drags me up to my feet. I don't make a sound. Not giving him the satisfaction.

'Lock her in the cellar,' he bellows at the bloke who dresses him and cleans up after him. 'I'll send someone for the constable.'

'Elizabeth Bartlett,' the judge says to me. 'You are hereby found guilty of the theft of a gold watch and a silver pair of buckles out of the house of James Dogherty. You will be transported for seven years.'

The cell is freezing. I think it's warmer on the Dublin streets than in here. The other women in the cell are sitting close to each other to keep warm. One of them uses her finger to signal I should join them. Not much choice. I either sit near them, or freeze to death. Maybe I should freeze to death. Might be easier in the long run.

Franny sent her mam to the prison with me stuff. I'm surprised her mam didn't run off with it. Seems she got better with the medicine. Franny's mam hands over my woollen over-coat. I've had it since I was twelve, when I left home to work in big houses. The coat is too small, but I'll be able to put my arms in and cover myself with it. She gives me a pair of boots I haven't seen before. Says they are Franny's and Franny wants me to have them.

I've been in this cell, in this Kilmainham Gaol, for months. We can hear the birds singing outside, so I figure it must be getting nearer springtime. No one has been to see me since Franny's mam. My own mam hasn't come, neither has Franny. They have their own troubles and don't want to be burdened with mine. Some girls have died. One of them was left in the cell for three days before they took her body away. We took it in turns at night to keep the rats from eating her. She looked real young, much younger than me.

It's called the *Marquis Cornwallis*, the ship they are putting us on. They've made us take a bath in a barrel, they've cut our hair back to nothing and put us in clothes that don't fit. But the clothes are clean, and I don't stink anymore. The whispers around the ship are that we're going to New South Wales. I never heard of it. They say it's going to take months to get there.

The guards feel us up while they're pushing us into our cells. The women who complain get a fist to the back of the head. I don't complain. I'm used to it. In the places I worked at in Dublin the masters of the house did the same to us girls. Same as slaves we were.

The cell on this ship is better than the prison cell in Kilmainham. At least we have a bunk each, so we are off the floor. Rats can climb, but it'll be easier to whack them off.

They tell us not to jump into bed with any sailors or guards, or members of the New South Wales Corp. Looking around at them while they gawk at us, I don't see myself rushing into their arms.

We've been sailing for about ten days, and some of the girls start slinking away at night and sneaking back before the sun comes up. I grabbed Shirley by the arm one night when she tiptoed past my bunk. She didn't yell out but bit my hand. I didn't let go.

'What do ye want?' she snarled at me.

'Where you going?'

She says she's not telling me. She says that where's she's going, they don't want no thieves. I twist my hand on her arm so that her skin burns. She's quite chatty after that. Seems she and some of the other girls are giving the privates of the New South Wales Corp their attention, and in return they're getting better and more food. I jump down off my bunk and tell her I'm going with her. My stomach's been grumbling for months.

He's all right, the private. His name's William; he's kind to me. Says his mam was from Dublin and he misses her voice. Liked to listen to me talking. He's not rough in the bed like the masters of the houses always were. And after, he always takes me back to the cell, so I won't get bothered by one of the disgusting guards. He says he's made it clear to them that I belong to him. I'm not happy about belonging to him. But I belong to the King and he's sending me to the other side of the world, so I figure it don't matter much.

When I tell William I'm with child he shrugs his shoulders and says there's nothing he can do about it. He says he'll keep taking me to his bed, so I get proper food to eat while the baby grows inside me, but when we land in New South Wales, if I say he's the father, he'll deny it and I'll be flogged.

.   .   .

My belly is swelling and when we are herded off the *Marquis Cornwallis* at Sydney Cove I try my best to keep my dress in place to hide the growing infant. William catches my eye, looks for a moment, then turns away. I know I'm not the only one with child, to a member of the New South Wales Corp. We all try to hide what desperation for a good feed has done to us.

There's seventy Irish girls on the *Marquis Cornwallis,* and we stand before the commandant, or whatever high and mighty title he gives himself, cooking in the sun like a pot of soup on the fire. A corporal from the New South Wales Corp wanders around looking us up and down. I'm one of the eight he tells to move to the side. My legs have trouble taking me where he says I have to go; they're expecting the ground to move like the sea.

Herding us like sheep away from the others, he tells us we'll be in Sydney Cove a couple of days and then we're being shipped off to Norfolk Island. That might as well be the moon as far as we know. He tells us cos we're Irish, we'll know how to weave the flax that grows on the Island, into cloth to make sails. We look at each other and raise our eyebrows. I don't know how to weave, and I'm pretty sure the girls standing near me don't either. But I'm not saying anything. I'm a slave, I have no rights. We all stay quiet.

9

Norfolk Island 1796

I've not seen anything this beautiful in my life. My baby will be born in paradise. I expect to see leprechauns or elves or faeries peeking from behind those magnificent trees. Me and two other girls put our heads back and take in the sky. It's bluer than I've ever seen. Bluer than the sky over the ocean on our journey. There are no clouds. The air is fresh, and tastes like the quince jam the cook used to let us have in the master's kitchen. I never thought air could have a taste, but this air does.

The men in the New South Wales Corp on this island don't push us, they wait while we walk behind, taking in the beauty. We're put in cabins. Not cells. There's four of us to a cabin. It's hot, but not suffocating like Sydney. There's a breeze coming through the windows. We each have our own bed, and there's a fire and a table with four chairs. There's some food on the table, and they tell us to cook it and look after ourselves. We share the cooking and sit down, the four of us, to eat like civilised women. At a table. We even have forks and spoons.

'They haven't given us knives,' I laugh. 'Wonder why they don't trust us with knives?'

We have a chuckle about that and tell each other our names and the stories of how we ended up on Norfolk Island.

After the best night's sleep I've had in years, there's a banging on the door and a bellowing voice tells us to get up and report to the middle of the settlement. We take longer than we should. We take time for a wash and to eat the rest of the bread, salted pork, and carrots. Carrots. Been a long time since I'd had a fresh carrot. The next banging on the door sees it swing wide and a red-faced English soldier straddles the opening and orders us to get to the meeting.

They're assigning us to settlers. This is the first time since I took the blame for Franny, that something has scared me. I'm with child and I've got no idea what it means to be assigned to a settler. Does it mean I'll be the property of some old man who'll have his way with me and treat me as bad as the masters of the houses in Dublin? I'll jump off one of them cliffs that runs along the edge of this Norfolk Island before I'll do that again.

They tell four of us to get up on the back of a cart with our stuff. None of us has much in the way of stuff, so it doesn't take long for us to settle. There's a bullock pulling, and a horse tied to the back of the cart: it's walking with its head down, staring at the ground its feet are treading on. Turning to the girl next to me, Mary, I say the horse looks broken and sad, like the way I'm feeling.

The driver hears me and turns to look at us. 'That horse is going to a settler who'll look after her. A settler who's earned his freedom. If you work hard you can earn your freedom too and have a good life. A couple of you look like you'll be convicts for a long while.'

Facing the front, he flicks the reins on the bullock's back.

The baby kicks me with a force that takes my breath away. 'I don't think the babe likes his mammy being a convict,' I say to Mary. 'I don't much like it either.'

Mary's the third one to get offloaded from the cart. I could see her hands shaking as she crumpled her dress to climb down with some dignity. A man and woman came out of a house that had solid walls, a roof, two chimneys and a front verandah. The man waves, the cart driver waves back, then gets down to greet the couple. I wanted to reach out and grab Mary and drag her back onto the cart, so we could huddle and be miserable together.

'Greetin's ta ye Thomas,' the man says to the driver. 'Ye've brought fer us a hard workin' lass 'ave ye?'

Mary moves her head to look at me, grinning. The man has a Dublin accent. He introduces himself to Mary as Patrick Connell. She curtsies like a good servant and tells him her name.

'Tis me wife, Elizabeth,' he says, 'she'll take ye and get ye sorted.'

Mary waves to me. Thomas flicks the reins on the bullock's back, and we trundle down the track to my place of servitude.

'It's your turn now,' the driver Thomas says as he pulls the bullock to a stop. 'You got lucky. You got Mr Cullen.'

I don't know how a person can think someone like me is lucky. I'm with child, I'm a slave on an island no one else in the world knows anything about, and I'm about to be handed over to a new master. For seven years.

A tall, strong looking older man strides out of a handsome house and makes his way to the cart. He shakes Thomas's hand and calls to a man working in the stable to untie the old horse and look after her. Then as if an afterthought, he turns to me. Taking off his hat, he gives a little bow and says his name is James Bryan Cullen and I'm welcome on his farm in Queenborough Path, Norfolk Island. I tell him my name's Elizabeth Bartlett and I'm pleased to meet him. I don't think he believes me. I don't believe me either.

'Go on into the house, Miss Bartlett. Have a wash and change your clothes if you want. There are women's clothes in a cupboard in the bedroom at the end of the hall. That's your room. You should find something that fits.'

My feet won't move. My brain is telling them to go, one in front of the other, but they're not listening. This man's being nice, talking to me like I'm a person. There's got to be a catch.

'Is everything all right?' he asks.

I nod that it is, but me feet still won't move. I start shaking. Can't stop. Any minute he's going to slap me across the back of my head.

'It's all right, Miss Bartlett,' he says to me so quiet I can hardly hear him. 'I'm not going to hurt you. You do a good day's work, and we'll get along just fine. We'll talk about your duties when you're cleaned up, fed and had a good night's sleep. Off you go.' He walks off, leaving me to make my feet move.

Taking a deep breath I got my feet to obey my brain and walk towards the house. The door was open. I stepped inside and wrapped my arms around myself, it felt like the house was giving me a hug. It smelled like old leather and pine needles. For the first time since Franny's eyes begged me to take the blame for her stealing, the tears run down my face. I don't wipe them away.

The house has a kitchen and a parlour and two bedrooms. Not as grand as the house I worked at in Dublin, but it's big, well made, and comfortable. I find the room Mr Cullen said would be mine. It has a sideboard with a wash bowl, a new piece of soap and a jug of fresh water. There's a towel folded real nice like and put over the side of the wash bowl. One wall has a cupboard, and a window that looks over the greenest grass that reminds me of the farms around Dublin. A big, soft looking bed is against the wall on the other side. The bed has two pillows, and a quilt that looks like the sunrise and sunset have been trapped in its fabric. I use the new bar of soap to wash my face, hands and arms in the water and dry myself with the clean towel.

Sitting on the edge of the bed looking out the window, I'm thinking I might try out the pillows and the quilt.

10

Norfolk Island October 1796

'I've never seen any creature more frightened and yet head-strong in my life,' Cullen said to the convict assigned to him as a farm labourer. 'She's with child. Her story will be interesting. No doubt we'll learn more about Miss Elizabeth Bartlett over supper.'

The house was quiet and the fire out when Cullen and his labourer returned for supper. Obvious to both men that the new addition was asleep, they fell into their familiar routine and prepared the evening meal.

'Make enough for the new miss?' asked the convict. Cullen nodded.

The mainstay of the evening meal since Anne Coombes had left was bread, often stale, corn, dried beef or pork and a big mug of sweet tea. 'I hope she can cook,' Cullen said as he put the plates on the table.

'Yes, I can cook. Is that all you want me for? To cook and clean?' Elizabeth said as she sauntered into the kitchen.

Almost choking on a piece of dry bread, Cullen laughed at

the young woman's bravado. 'That's a start.' He noticed how different her appearance was to that of Anne Coombes when she arrived on the farm: her hair fought with her hands as she tried to brush her long locks off her face, her dress looked as if she'd slept in it with one sleeve rolled up and the other down. 'Come and sit down, Elizabeth. You must be hungry. This is my farm labourer, Edward. You can call him Ed.' Cullen watched Ed's eyes follow Elizabeth's walk from the doorway to the table. Something to monitor.

Cullen didn't ask Elizabeth questions about herself while she devoured her food and devour it she did. He wondered when she last had a decent meal. He didn't like the way Ed looked at her, and would wait until the convict had retired to his small cottage between the house and the stable before engaging the young woman in conversation. Offering her another corn cob and more dried beef, Cullen filled up a mug with tea and asked Elizabeth how many spoons of sugar she wanted. She swallowed the food she'd been chewing and looked at Cullen with eyes that pierced his soul. 'How many sugars?' he asked again.

'I, I, I, don't know. I've never been asked if I want sugar and no man has ever made be a mug of tea.'

'I'll put in two. That should be enough.' Cullen stirred the tea with a spoon larger than should have been used, and put it in front of his new house guest.

'Thanks be to you,' Elizabeth said as she put her hands around the hot mug and sipped the contents gingerly. 'Is Ed a convict?' she asked after the first few sips.

'Yes.'

'Where does he sleep then?'

'There's a small cottage between this house and the stable. That's his quarters. He usually eats with me; it saves us worrying about him having enough food in his place.'

Cullen noticed Elizabeth eyeing Ed up and down.

'Don't you get any nasty, funny, ideas Mr Ed. I's might be a convict too, and even though I'm with child, I'm no whore, and you won't be thinkin' you can treat me like one. Got it?'

Ed nodded, bade Cullen goodnight and left for his cottage.

'Sorry Mr Cullen. Don't mean to be rude, but I didn't like the way he was lookin' at me. Gave me the creeps.'

'I noticed.'

After helping Cullen clear the table and wash and dry the dishes, Elizabeth asked if she had permission to go to bed.

Seeing the dark rings under her eyes he told her to sleep well.

11

The sun was shining bright through the window when I woke up. Don't know how long I'd been sleeping. Felt like a hundred years. My stomach was rumbling. The bedroom door was shut, it didn't look as if anyone had been in the room. When I remembered this was the first day of my convict assignment for this old Cullen fella I jumped out of bed. I was busting for a wee but had to put clothes on first. I pulled my dress over my head, pulled on my boots, and opened the bedroom door. I smelled food. Walking in a hurry to the kitchen, I saw the old Cullen fella standing over the fire stirring something. 'Excuse me,' I said loud like. 'Where's the privy?'

He turned around quick. I think I gave him a fright. Smiling at me he said it was outside. He must take me for some idiot. I know, I didn't see it inside, I wanted to scream at him. I was crossing my legs. Opening the door he told me to follow him and he pointed to a timber construction up back of the house. I nodded, picked up me dress and ran like the devil. All the time worried I'd wet myself. These were the only clothes I had.

Feeling much better I walked back into the kitchen. He was putting food on the table and there was a plate and a tin mug.

He asked if I felt better. What did he care? Thinking I'd better be polite I told him I did, and said thank you. Telling me I shouldn't let the food get cold, he said to sit at the table. What do I make of this man? Is he going to suddenly turn all nasty like? Is he going to want to have his way with me, even if I am with child? He's got this calm feeling about him. Relaxed and comfortable. It doesn't seem to bother him that I'm a convict and he's my master. Pulling out a chair I sit down where he told me to. '

Help yourself,' says. 'I used to have a woman living here with me and she left behind a couple of things. They're in the cupboard in your room. I think they'll fit; she was a big woman. When you've eaten and got yourself washed and dressed you can come to the stable. I'll show you around the farm.'

I stared at him. I knew my mouth was open. No man ever in my life, not ever, has spoken to me as nice as he was doing.

'It'll be all right, Miss Bartlett,' he said while he grabbed his hat and pulled on his boots. I stared at the door long after he'd gone.

With no one watching me I shovelled down the bread and eggs like I hadn't eaten for three years. The tea was hot and sweet. I belched like an old farm hand, because I could. No one was watching. Before I checked out the clothes my new master told me to look at I cleared the table, washed the dishes and put things away in the tidy cupboard he had running along the wall. Although it wasn't cold, I stoked the fire, so it'd be ready for dinner time. All I could think about really was my next meal. The infant gave me a kick, it made my dress move. He must have been thinking about good food too.

There were two dresses, petticoats, stockings, a hat and a thick woollen jacket thing that I couldn't give a name to. They smelled liked they'd been washed and hung in the sunshine for a couple of days. My guess was the old man had done just that. Still I worried what he was up to. The dresses and petticoats were a bit short because my belly stuck out like a boil on the bum of a lazy lord. But they fitted. He was right, she must've been a big woman. Looking more presentable and with my face washed and hair brushed and put up, I went outside to find my way to the stable like I'd been ordered.

'Good morning, again, Miss Bartlett,' he says to me all cheerful and pleasant. 'I see the clothes fit well enough.'

I couldn't help myself, I let him have it. 'Why are you so nice to me?' I yelled. 'I'm your servant, slave, convict. I'm waiting for you to throw me on the ground and have your way with me, or to hit me for something I've done wrong. So just get on with it so I know what life's going to be like.'

He walked over to me and I got ready to protect my head from a wallop.

'This is how life is, Miss Bartlett. I'm not interested in having my way with you. Nor am I interested in hitting you when you do the wrong thing. I've had my freedom for six years, Miss Bartlett. I don't take being a free man lightly, and I won't inflict punishment on another person just because it was inflicted on me.'

My mouth fell open just as a gust of wind swept by. I could hear my mother's voice telling me my face would stay like that if the wind changed. I closed my mouth. 'Then what do you want from me, Mr Cullen?'

'You can start by looking after the vegetable garden. That's where we get most of our food. Do you know how to look after hens? Because they need fresh water every day, and to be let out of the hen house to forage. No predators here except the birds and the birds keep away if people are around. There are bugs on the vegetables, you'll have to pick off the ones the hens don't eat. And if you are able to cook dinner and supper for yourself and me and Ed, I would be grateful. I'll do breakfast. I suppose there's all the other jobs required to run a house. The more you can do, the more I can work on the farm and produce more food and in the end, money. Is that all right with you?'

Because I couldn't think of anything else to say or do, I nodded. He tipped his hat, and went straight on back to whatever job he was doing before I yelled at him. I lifted up the fat woman's dress that I was wearing and marched back to the house. He was watching me. I know he was.

First thing I did when I got back to the house was see what the hens were doing. They were huddling around the door to the hen house, waiting to be let out. There was eight of them. I looked around for the rooster, because they are nasty rotten things. No rooster. The hens fell over each other trying to get into the garden. He didn't ask me to collect eggs, but I looked anyway, and there were eight. Clever little girls, all laying an egg.

Standing up straight and taking deep breaths I put my hands on the lower part of my back. It ached. The infant was getting bigger, kicking me heaps and making my skin stretch. I had to use my knees when I bent to pick up the hens' water, I couldn't bend in the middle anymore. With the hens sorted and the eggs in my pockets, I went back into the house. I wondered if I was the lady of the house and laughed at myself. 'You're a convict,' I said out loud.

I put the eggs on the kitchen table, making sure they didn't roll away, and while no-one else was in the house I thought I'd do some snooping. Where was the old man's room? It wasn't hard to find, there were only two bedrooms. He had a great big bed in the middle of the room, with a quilt on it like the one on my bed. It was neat and tidy like the rest of the house. His clothes were put away in cupboards and on shelves and his washbasin and water jug were shiny and clean. A funny warm feeling swept over me. If he looked after himself and the house without a woman to order around, perhaps he is going to be alright.

Before I went to the kitchen to see what food was available for cooking dinner, I went back into the room Mr Cullen had given me. The bed looked as if I'd been wrestling the devil all night, and my clothes, wet from the day before, were still in a heap on the floor. I grinned at how odd this was, the old man clean and tidy and me, a mess. I fluffed up the pillows, pulled up the quilt and straightened it, picked up my clothes and carried them to the kitchen. There was a lean to off the side of the kitchen that had a big metal tub sitting over a grate that had logs under it. 'That's clever. You fill the tub up with cold water and light the fire underneath to heat the water.' I shuddered when I remembered the number of young ones at home, scalded to death or scarred for life when hot water, being carried by an older brother or sister, or their mother, spilled on them.

The parlour had two chairs either side of the fireplace, glass in the window and a funny looking rug on the floor. I bent down to touch it, it was coarse and smelled like sheep, but finished off really well and looked good in the middle of the room. I wondered where people sat if he had more than one visitor in here. Not like the parlours I was used to cleaning in the big houses in Dublin. This was nicer.

Back in the kitchen I explored the cupboards and shelves. Along one wall there were shelves stacked with dried beef and pork, eggs, flour, sugar, tea, yeast, two loaves of bread, and his pots and pans. On the other wall, under the window, he had a long bench with a tub half buried in the timber. Under that was a cupboard that had all the fresh vegetables from his garden. There were potatoes, onions, corn cobs, bags of peas and beans and what smelled like cabbage. Not a lover of cabbage, but it can be covered up in stews and things. He even had bags of carrots. No wonder he and that creepy Ed looked healthy. 'Looks like you're going to be fed properly,' I said to the baby as I rubbed my belly.

I took one of the cooking pots to the creek that ran at the back of the vegetable garden bent down, and half-filled it with water. I think I'll ask him about putting a tub of some sort near the door so that Ed fellow can fill it up with water from the creek, save me dragging myself down there a hundred times a day. I tipped most of the water into the tub that was used to wash the dishes. I stoked the fire that was still smouldering and put the pot on the cradle that sat over it. Figuring I'd be cooking for three people, I chopped an onion, two carrots, peeled and chopped three potatoes, pulled the husks off a corn cob and used a knife to get the little yellow kernels to give up their hold. I left the cabbage on the shelf. Slicing off a piece of dried pork, I chopped that up too. Standing back to look at my handiwork, I had a giggle at what Franny would think now. She'd be thinking I was already dead, I'm sure.

The pork and vegetables went into the pot on the fire, and I found a lid that fitted. I didn't know the time, but knew east and west. I thought Mr Cullen and that Ed would probably be in around noon, so I guessed where the sun would be then. Plenty of time for the food to be ready.

While the food cooked on the fire, I wandered outside. The air had a zing to it, crisp and clean. You could smell the sea, the great big trees up on the hills behind the house and the grass. You could smell the grass. I'd never smelled grass before. The hens were scratching around the vegetables pecking at little bugs they knocked off the leaves. There was wheat and corn growing in two paddocks off the side of the stable. I couldn't see Mr Cullen or that Ed fellow. The sun hung like a yellow circle in the middle of a bright blue painting. No clouds, just the blue sky and the sun. I could see glimpses of the ocean beyond the hills, it was the same colour as the sky. This place might be the other end of the world, but I'd never seen magic like it. It wrapped itself around me like a mother hugging her tired child.

'Miss Bartlett, Miss Bartlett,' I heard a man yelling out, but no one called me Miss Bartlett, I was Lizzie or girl. I wondered who he was calling to. 'Miss Bartlett, are you all right?' I opened my eyes and saw Mr Cullen standing over me. Took a minute to work out what was going on. Then I burst out laughing. I'd laid down on the grass that smelled so sweet and must have nodded off. He thought I'd died or something. That would have been a nuisance; replacing a convict on her first day.

'I'm fine. Must have nodded off. Sorry. Dinner should be ready.' He put out his hand to help me up. Because I couldn't bend in the middle I needed the assistance, but it was still embarrassing.

He sliced the bread and I put plates and forks on the table. He took my plate and walked over to the fire and scooped a big spoonful of stew onto it. He put it on the table and told me to sit down and eat. He did his and Ed's plates. We sat at the table, him on one side, me on the other, and Ed at one end. I wanted to laugh and cry at the same time. Two days ago I was terrified about what was going to happen to me and the baby, and here I was sitting in a strange man's house, eating dinner with a fork like a civilised woman. A dinner I'd cooked.

12

Cullen watched Elizabeth shovelling the food into her mouth. He well remembered what it was like to have that first good meal. For him, the first one was six years after his arrest. It was here on Norfolk Island, when Richard Morgan invited him to dinner.

Her cheeks turned apple red when she noticed him watching her.

'Must be the fresh air on Norfolk Island. I ate like that when I first got here. Richard Morgan had me to dinner, and I made a fool of myself. Couldn't eat quickly enough. Richard laughed at me. I know what it's like to be hungry for a decent meal, Miss Bartlett.'

Not stopping to take in his comments, Elizabeth finished the food without lifting her head. Cullen stacked up his and Ed's plates, pushed his chair out, nodded to Ed, smiled at Elizabeth, and made his way out of the kitchen. 'That was a good dinner, Miss Bartlett. Thank you.'

Ed followed him, leering at her as he strolled past.

'I don't like the way you're looking at Miss Bartlett, Ed,' Cullen pointed to a scythe leaning against the wall of the storage shed indicating Ed should pick it up. 'Get onto the wheat and make a start with the harvest while I harness the horse. Be mindful I'm in charge of that young woman as much as I am you. If you make advances and she rejects you, leave her alone.'

'What's a man supposed to do?' Ed whined. 'It's not as if there's plenty of women to go around. A convict like me has no chance.'

'Easy way out of that predicament, Ed. Work hard, keep your head down, earn your freedom and find yourself a wife.'

Uneasy at Ed's quick, unsavoury response to a young woman arriving on the farm, Cullen decided to watch him carefully when Elizabeth Bartlett was near.

Sitting on the steps that led to the verandah at the front of the house, Elizabeth watched Cullen and Ed tramp towards her across the cleared land that surrounded the house. She'd put the hens in the coop and secured them for the night, taken the milking goat and her kid into the barn and set the table for supper.

'Good evening Miss Bartlett. I trust your first full day on my farm has been a pleasant one. Ed and I are looking forward to supper.' Cullen took of his hat and slapped it against his thigh, dust sprinkled into the sunbeams that floated over the short plants growing in front of the verandah. 'Ed and I will wash the dust of our hands, faces and arms and join you inside.'

Elizabeth used the railing on the steps to hoist herself up, and went into the kitchen to stoke the fire for the kettle. 'There is bread, cheese, pickles and dried pork to eat,' she said as the two men made their way into the kitchen.

'We'd just about eat anything, Miss Bartlett.' Cullen put a thick slice of bread on Elizabeth's plate and another on Ed's before putting one on his own. 'If you find the larder wanting,

Miss Bartlett, please make a list of what you think is missing, or what you need to run the household and I'll see to getting it from Sydney Town.'

Standing to clear the table, Elizabeth collected the plates and cutlery and took them to the sideboard. While she waited for the kettle to boil for hot water for the dishes, and to make tea, she wiped the timber table with a damp cloth, collecting the breadcrumbs in her hand before they fell on the floor.

Cullen said he was going into the parlour to read, and asked Ed to come with him to stoke the fire. Watching Ed turn to look back at Elizabeth, Cullen didn't think it would be long before Ed made a move on the young woman.

'Join us when you're ready, Miss Bartlett.'

Putting tea leaves in the pot and filling it with boiling water, Elizabeth looked up at Cullen. 'Join you where?'

'In the parlour, Miss Bartlett. I like to read the newspapers even though they are months old. Sometimes I get old books that have made their way from England via Sydney.' He didn't ask her if she knew how to read. The furrow on her brow told him she didn't. 'The house could do with a woman's touch. If you enjoy needle craft you might find some time to sew curtains, or even clothes for yourself or your infant, or knit for the colder months. There's always plenty to keep us busy.'

Leaving Elizabeth to her thoughts, Cullen took up his position by the fire in the parlour, newspaper open, ready to absorb the news from the other side of the world.

Three china cups lined up on the table, Elizabeth poured tea into each one, leaving room at the top to stir the sugar without spilling the tea. She carried two cups into the parlour and put them on the table next to Cullen's chair.

'Ed will get his own cup, and the lemon cake I made the other day. Sit down, Miss Bartlett.'

Elizabeth picked up a cup for herself and sat on the small settee which hugged the windowsill.

'That's a good place to sit in the morning on a winter's day. The sun fills the room until almost midday.'

Returning with his cup and the cake, Ed moved to sit next to Elizabeth. Cullen noticed she moved away from the man pressing herself into the side of the settee.

'Have some cake, Miss Bartlett, I made it from the lemons in the orchard.' Cullen moved to the settee and offered the plate to Elizabeth, and Ed. 'We'll talk about your tasks here on the farm when Ed retires to his room in the stable.'

Bidding Cullen and Elizabeth good night, Ed made his way through the kitchen and outside toward the stable.

'Why does he sleep in the stable?' Elizabeth asked.

Finishing his tea and collecting crumbs from his jacket to throw into the fire, Cullen explained. 'Ed has been here three years. When he arrived the house had two rooms: a bedroom and the kitchen/parlour. A woman lived with me at the time, so Ed made himself a comfortable space in the stable. Adding the rooms didn't make a difference, he preferred his own space.'

'What tasks did you want to talk to me about, Mr Cullen?'

Cullen told Elizabeth about the bugs that ate the vegetables and the damage the salty winds off the ocean caused to the citrus trees.

She listened carefully, making mental notes about how her days would unfold.

13

I keep waiting for the axe to fall, for Mr Cullen's good humour to pass and him to start getting nasty with me. I've never worked for a man who thinks about how I'm doing. He asks every morning if I slept well, and tells me what a wonderful dinner or supper I cooked for him and Ed. Something's got to happen. I don't want to let my guard down and not be ready, so I nod and smile and thank him, but watch for the signs of him being about to grab or hit me. But Ed is the one who has that look in his eyes, and I think Mr Cullen is making sure he leaves me alone.

It's getting harder to get down on my hands and knees to pick the grubs off the vegetables. The hens don't eat the grubs that do the most damage, and if I don't keep on top of it, we won't have any fresh vegetables to eat, except corn. I imagine we'll get sick of that pretty quickly. This morning after breakfast while the dew was still damp on the ground and on the cabbage and peas and beans, I got down on my hands and knees to crawl along and pick off caterpillars. I didn't hear him come up behind me, but I could hear him breathing really fast. Turning to look at who I thought was Mr Cullen, I saw Ed force a smile onto his face that showed his brown, broken teeth. I hadn't noticed his teeth before.

Let me help you up,' he said.

I told him I was fine on the ground, I had lots of work to do, and asked what he wanted. He knelt down next to me and said 'You, I want you. Now get up or I'll drag you up.'

I just looked up at him. I'd been eyeing off Mr Cullen waiting for him to attack, and it was always Ed I needed to fear. I told him I wasn't getting up, that I was busy. I turned back to the caterpillars. He pulled my hair until I found my way to my feet. Screaming for help wasn't any good, Mr Cullen was right down the other end of the farm setting up scarecrows to keep the parrots away from the crops. He must've sent Ed back to get something.

'Get into the stable. Hurry up. I haven't got all day.'

He pushed me in the middle of the back all the way from the vegetable garden to his space in the stable. Shoving me onto some bales of hay, he undid his trousers and stood over me. 'Lift up your dress you whore,' he yelled.

The baby due any week, I don't know how he thought he was going to get anywhere near me to have his way. I didn't move. He slapped my face and put his hand over my mouth. Must've thought Mr Cullen might hear. Frightened for the infant, I didn't know what to do. In Ireland I would've kicked him in the groin and run off while he was struggling for breath and doubled over in pain. He pulled up my dress and yelled at me to open my legs. I took too long, he hit me on the side of my head with his fist. Pushing my legs apart, he thrust himself into me over and over. Apart from Stephen on the *Marquis Corn-wallis* coming to New South Wales, every man I'd come across in my life treated me like this. I still thought Mr Cullen would too. Ed put his whole weight on my belly to get a better position to finish what he'd started. I screamed in pain; the infant struggled against the pressure. It didn't take him long to be done.

'Don't say anything to Cullen, or I'll slit your belly in the middle of the night and kill both of you.'

He pulled up his pants and turned to leave. Mr Cullen stood in the door of the stable.

'I wondered why you were taking so long to get the mallet,' he said disgust spreading all over his face. His eyes turned from grey to black when he looked down at me.

'You forget I'm the Constable for this district, Ed. After you've been flogged, you'll be sent back to New South Wales. Looks like it'll be a long time before you get your freedom.'

Mr Cullen grabbed a pitchfork from near the door and pointed it at Ed, forcing him to back away against the wall. 'I'll help you in a minute, Miss Bartlett,' he said. He shoved Ed and told him to put his hands behind his back. He tied Ed's wrists with so many knots I didn't think anyone would ever get them undone. Forcing Ed to his knees, Mr Cullen came to help me up. While I was slapping my clothes to get the hay off, I noticed blood on the floor. Mr Cullen noticed too.

'Go to the house, Miss Bartlett. I'm taking this convict straight to the cells in Sydney Town. I'll get one of the women to hurry along to look in on you.'

16th July 1796

I don't know how long it took. Seemed like hours and hours. The sun had moved in the sky and was thinking about lowering itself onto the horizon when Kitty Morgan let herself into the house. She found me in the parlour on the floor. My pains started after Ed used his fists to push himself off my belly.

Kitty made a gasping sound and put her hand over her mouth. She helped me up and we walked very slowly to my bed. The pains were every few minutes and I felt like my insides were going to explode. Kitty got hot water ready, and clean towels and held my hand and told me everything would be all right.

My son made his way into the world just as the day ended and the night stretched its arms over the grass and trees. Kitty wrapped him up and rubbed his back until he cried. He didn't look right to me. He was a funny colour. A bit blue. When I asked, Kitty said he was cold and she kept rubbing his back, trying to make him cry more. After a few minutes my son let out an enormous cry and Kitty, seeming satisfied he was doing what he was supposed to, gave him to me to hold. Get him sucking straight away she said as she helped put him to my breast.

I looked down on my new son, he had dark hair like his father and clenched his fists like a fighter. Kitty asked what I was going to call him. 'William,' I told her. 'After his father.'

Mr Cullen sat by my bed on a chair he'd brought from the kitchen. His eyes were puffy and red, and his face was the colour of the ash that settles in the fireplace.

'I'm so sorry, Miss Bartlett. It is my job to provide your protection and I let you down. All I can offer is that Ed will be punished with a flogging and more time on his sentence.'

This was the first time in my life a man who'd raped me was going to be punished. I laughed, 'That was a long time coming.' Mr Cullen's eyebrows knitted together and some of the grey from his face slipped away and was replaced with pink. When I told him why I was laughing, Mr Cullen patted my hand, smiled at William and left the room.

Kitty's husband, Richard Morgan, sent one of his workers to collect his wife and for the first time since I arrived five months earlier, Mr Cullen and I were the only adults on the farm.

In all my days I'd never, ever had someone bring me a cup of tea and something to eat while I was in bed. Before Mammy sent me to work when I was twelve, I cleaned and looked after the little ones. I don't remember a time when my day didn't start before the sun rose. Mr Cullen put a cup of tea on the little table by the side of my bed.

'I put in two sugars, Miss Bartlett,' he said. 'Hope that's all right.'

I nodded that it was. Didn't' know what else to do. This was unknown territory. He left the room and came back with sliced bread, cheese and salted beef. Told me he thought I would need my strength to look after little William, then he disappeared again. I was thinking about how I was going to manage eating bread and cheese and drink tea while I was holding a new baby when Mr Cullen came in with a crib he'd made. It was as if the moon had leaped out of the sky and put itself behind Mr Cullen's head and shone through his face. His eyes sparkled and his mouth was in the biggest smile I'd seen since Mary heard the Dublin accent of her new master.

'I've been working on it for a few weeks. In secret. I wanted to surprise you.'

Surprise me he did. I started blubbering like an eight year old boy being sent to the coal mines for the first time. The tears kept coming; pouring from my eyes faster than I could wipe them off my cheeks.

'Don't you like it?'

I squeaked out I loved it, snuffling and sobbing when I saw he'd put a new blanket in the crib. Holding William out to him I nodded, and Mr Cullen took my new baby boy and put him in his new little bed.

It saddened me a bit to think William would never see his son. But there are probably lots of girls like me around the world that men like William have got with child never to recognise them or be part of their lives. Mr Cullen would be a good father, but I think he might be too old. He's got the strength and body of a young man, but I reckon he's about fifty.

He was still standing looking at the baby when I finally stopped blubbering.

'He makes lots of noises. Is he supposed to?'

I told him babies make lots of funny sounds. I'd looked after the babes Mammy had since I was five. Two of them died because they were too cold. Mammy didn't have enough milk to make them fat enough to keep themselves warm. William won't be cold or hungry, not on Mr Cullen's farm on Norfolk Island.

November 1796

James Bryan Cullen finished the edges of the tiny coffin he'd made from one of the felled Norfolk Island pines on his property. He lined the small casket with a blanket from the infant's crib. Miss Bartlett had called the child William after the marine who fathered him on the voyage from England. Although not uncommon for infants to die soon after birth, Cullen worried that Elizabeth seemed exceptionally distraught. Because he was born on Norfolk Island, she said she hadn't considered his death a possibility. Infants died in Dublin and London, not Norfolk Island.

Carrying the coffin into the house, he set it down in front of the hearth and stepped quietly toward Miss Bartlett's room. Running his hands through his hair to flatten it he waited for an answer to his knock on the door.

'Come in.'

The door squeaked as he pushed it inwards reminding him that he should oil the hinges. Elizabeth sat in the chair next to the fireplace, still cradling her deceased infant. She had been there since the child died twenty-four hours earlier. 'It's time to go, Miss Bartlett. We must take William to the cemetery. Our friends and neighbours will be waiting.'

She offered no resistance as he bent forward and took the baby from her arms. His little body, stiff and cold, was wrapped in a blanket she'd made from the one on her own bed. Cullen took the baby to the kitchen and put him in the coffin as gently as if he were still alive. He kissed the tips of his fingers and touched the child's forehead 'Rest in peace, little one.' Tears that had no reason to fall for the last seven years, coursed down his cheeks.

Elizabeth didn't make a sound on the way to Emily Bay. She sat on the wagon with the tiny coffin tied on the back, occasionally looking over her shoulder as if to reassure herself it wasn't a dream.

She stood by the hole Cullen had dug the day before and watched while her infant son's coffin was lowered into the ground. She had nothing to add to the words Cullen offered at her son's graveside, nor to the comfort provided by Kitty Morgan and her husband, Richard.

Cullen left her standing next to her son's grave, looking over the stunning view from Emily Bay towards the sapphire blue ocean. He sat on the wagon until she was ready to leave.

'I'll make a headstone for his grave,' he said, looking to her for some reinforcement. Elizabeth nodded without comment.

Cullen didn't know how long he should allow Elizabeth Bartlett to grieve before expecting her to continue with her duties around the house and the farm. He hadn't anticipated her return to work the day after the funeral.

'I'm happy to give your more time, Miss Bartlett, to grieve your son and recover,' he said as she prepared breakfast the next morning.

'Thank you, no. What good would that do? It won't bring William back, and I need to keep my mind busy.'

Cullen nodded and thanked the convict woman assigned to him for being such a great help on the farm. Trudging off to the stable to harness the bullock for ploughing, he contemplated applying for another farm hand. An older man, like him, who wouldn't risk his freedom for the sake of a few minutes lying with a woman.

James Cullen chose the convict labourer carefully. He knocked back young men for fear they would harass Miss Bartlett, in favour of a man a bit younger than himself who seemed strong of character and body.

'Miss Bartlett this is Timothy.' Cullen introduced his new worker to Elizabeth. 'He's the new farm hand. Miss Bartlett is the housekeeper,' he said to Timothy and you will take heed of the things we discussed on the wagon ride from Sydney Town.'

Nodding at Elizabeth hoping she would understand the warning he'd given the new worker, Cullen indicated to Timothy that he should make his way out the door.

Spending some time showing Timothy around the farm, Cullen felt confident he'd made the right choice.

'When we've got the wheat and corn planted, we'll start an extension on the house. So you don't have to sleep in the stable for the length of your sentence.'

Timothy shook Cullen's hand and thanked him for his humanity, adding that it wasn't something he expected in the circumstances.

14

Norfolk Island 1798

None of the things that happened to me in my life before this moment could have prepared me for the way I felt about Mr Cullen. I wasn't sure if I loved him, because I've never been in love. But I admire and care for him. The kindness he showed after that Ed bastard raped me, how he looked after me when William was born, and everything he did when my little boy died, drew me to him. I've noticed his funny ways; things I didn't see when I first arrived. He turns his head on the side when he smiles and runs his right hand through his hair when he's fidgety about something. His blue eyes dance when he looks at me and he licks his lips and thanks me for every meal I prepare, even if it's not so wonderful. When I lie in bed at night, I wonder if he thinks anything more of me than as a useful convict to have around.

We were sitting on the front porch of the house looking over the grass to the edge of the cliffs, and the sunset that looks as if

God has taken all the paints in the world and swished them across the sky to make dozens of different colours, takes my breath away.

'It never fails to amaze, does it, Miss Bartlett?'

I tell him it doesn't matter how many sunsets I see on this island; they always amaze me.

'Does that mean when you are a free woman you are staying here?' he asks.

I haven't given any thought to what I'll do when I'm a free woman, I tell him. Adding that while I worked for him I didn't feel like a convict.

He pulled his chair closer to me and put his hand on mine. I didn't pull away, but I didn't encourage him either. The skin was dry and coarse but the strength in his hand brought comfort. Like the rest of him. We sat there without talking or moving until the earth on the horizon swallowed up the sun.

He held the door open for me when I went to go back into the house, telling me how nice I smelled as I walked past.

It's the peel from the lemons, I grate it and put it in the soap bars I make I said. He asked me to make some for him.

I lay awake most of the night fretting about telling James I was with child; worrying myself into a state about his reaction. Without thinking it through I told him over breakfast, before Timothy came into the kitchen. I said he'd need to add another room to the house, at least if he didn't want to send Timothy back to the stable. It will be nice for the baby to have its own room when it's bigger, I whispered, not taking my eyes off James' face.

'But I'm fifty-five. I'm an old man,' he blurted across the kitchen table.

Apparently that makes no difference, I said to him.

He moved around the table so fast I wasn't sure if I should

put my hands up for protection, or to embrace him. His arms went around my waist and he pulled me to him, purring that he was the happiest man on Norfolk Island.

My garden on Norfolk Island, yes my garden, had an abundant growth of chickpeas, cauliflower, cabbage, potatoes, green beans and citrus trees. The blood red soil grew anything I planted in it as long as I kept the bugs from devouring the plants when they poked up through the ground. The warm days and the rain, coming when it was needed, kept up a bountiful supply.

On a trip to Sydney Town one Wednesday, James brought home a goat. She was to give birth soon, judging by the size of her belly. He laughed when he gave me the rope that connected me and the goat, saying it was hard to know which had the biggest belly, the goat or me.

Watching him saunter off to tend to his horse I came to wonder about a world that led me to this life on Norfolk Island. The decision to take the blame for stealing the stuff from the master in Dublin was the best one I'd made in my life. The events that led me to be here with James, living on this island paradise, are etched in my soul as the best things to ever happen to me.

The first time James kissed me was months after William died. He tiptoed around me as if I would break if he touched me. One day I yelled at him that I was a convict and he my master; I wanted to know what he was afraid of.

'You've been through a lot,' he said, 'I don't want to upset you.'

I had to sit down I laughed so much. My head tilted back, then forward again, the tears streamed down my face. He just stood there, watching me. I think he wondered if I was going mad.

'Surely it doesn't matter what I've been through. I'm no-one, with nothing. The only good thing ever to happen in my life was to be sent here to this place, to be with you.'

Water filled his eyes and overflowed onto his cheeks. I could see them forming tracks on the dust on his face.

'Your tears are making your face dirtier,' I said.

He wiped his face saying they weren't tears, that his eyes were watering from the dust from the corn field.

Before I could start laughing again, he put his arms around my waist and pulled me to him. He's a lot taller than me and I craned my neck to see into his eyes. They were blue, like the ocean that surrounded Norfolk Island; they sparkled like the sun dancing on the waves. He leaned in and kissed me with the tenderness you dream about when you're lying with someone who is only interested in the sex. I kissed him back. When he gently pushed me away from him, I shivered. I wasn't cold, it was a strange feeling. He worried that he'd upset me, told me he was sorry. I put my hand over his mouth, leaned into him, moved my hand, and we kissed again. This time the shivering was replaced by a throbbing warmth between my legs. That was new.

Our life is blessed. I spend my days working in the garden: weeding, planting, pruning, harvesting and in the kitchen, cooking. I like cooking. I cooked when I lived at home with Mammy and remember most of what she taught me and what I learned from watching. James compliments the meals every time we eat dinner and supper. Seems he is happy to have someone cook for him doesn't matter so much what it is, as long as we can eat it.

His friends from the First Fleet, the ones who have been sent to Norfolk Island call in and we sometimes keep company with them and their wives. Abraham Hands is a pleasant man, but

Richard Morgan seems tense and high strung a lot of the time. His wife Kitty, he calls her his wife even though he is still married to someone else, is a few years older than me, was sent here as a convict and assigned to Morgan. Our stories are similar. Kitty has three children; they all have her last name because she and Richard aren't married. I haven't spoken to James about how that is going to affect our child's name. Kitty says that because I'm still a convict and there's no priest to marry us, the infant will be registered with my name. James won't be happy about that.

My pains started in the middle of the night. With no moon, the house was dark as a coal pit. James works hard and he's not as young as some. I tried to keep quiet, tried not to groan and moan while lying next to him. He needs his sleep. I wasn't that successful because he started to toss and turn. Getting up I wrapped a blanket around myself and made my way to the kitchen. The fire was still smouldering, so I stoked it and put more wood on it. I dragged a kitchen chair over near the fire, wrapped the blanket around myself, including my feet, and sat on the chair watching the flames. I didn't sit for very long, the pains in my back ran right along from one side to the other, sharp and deep. I couldn't lean forward, my belly was too big, so I stood up and paced up and down in front of the fire and around the kitchen table. I sat down between pains. When my waters broke I knew I should wake James.

With the help of one of the other women who had borne children on Norfolk Island, mine and James' son, came into the world as the sun rose and the cock crowed to herald the start of a new day. He was a good colour and started suckling greedily as soon as the midwife finished cleaning him up and cutting the chord. James stood next to our bed looking down at me and the baby as if he was the richest man in the world, and had just got richer.

James helped the midwife clean up the bed and when I was settled on the pillows, nursing our new baby, he showed the woman out and made me a cup of tea that was so sweet it warmed my insides all the way down.

'I want to name him John,' James said to me as he gave me the cup of tea. 'After my young friend who didn't make it.'

'I thought Stephen,' I said. 'My little brother who died was Stephen and my Pappy was Stephen.' Not meaning to turn on the tears to get his sympathy and to agree with me, I couldn't stop them running down my cheeks when I thought of my baby brother.

'If it means so much to you, we'll call him Stephen John,' he said kissing my cheek. Timothy can handle the farm today, I'll stay here with you and Stephen, make sure you're all right.'

I told him I would be fine, and to remember this was my second baby and I was young and strong. He insisted on staying.

It was lovely having James looking after me. He made sure the fires in the kitchen and the parlour were alight, and kept them burning through the day. It was September, but early spring on Norfolk Island still managed to have somewhat of a chill in the air. He brought me cups of sweet tea, and biscuits and busied himself baking bread and sorting the salted beef he'd brought back from Sydney Town.

He'd made a new crib for Stephen. The one he'd made for William he gave away to one of the other settlers. He didn't want me to have to look at it and think about the child I'd lost. After he stood holding Stephen for a while, he put him in his crib and helped me out of bed. I put my arms around him, buried my head in his chest and told him, for the first time, that I loved him. I'd never loved anyone the way I loved James. Kissing me all over my face, and wiping my tears, he told me he'd never loved anyone the way he loved me.

.   .   .

Stephen thrived. My milk kept him satisfied and the food I grew in the garden and that James bought from the Stores in Sydney Town, and traded with other settlers, kept us well fed.

The weather was getting warmer, so I could lay Stephen on a blanket on the ground in the shade while I worked in the vegetable garden. His little arms flayed about like he was swatting flies and his legs moved like he was practising how to walk in thin air. His chubby, pink cheeks and fat little arms and legs completed the picture of perfection. I had never seen a baby so healthy in Dublin. Looking up to the miraculous blue sky that covered our island home, I gave a prayer of thanks to God. I don't know if He listened me to, it's not like I prayed often, but I was truly grateful to be here with James and Stephen.

James roared to Timothy to come and get the horse and cart while he stomped across the yard to the garden. Pushing myself up and wiping my hands on the towel I had tied to my waist; I watched his red face and clenched fists get closer. I didn't ask what was wrong, I waited for him to speak first. He'd gone to arrange the sale of land and to purchase more; I wasn't expecting that to create such a scene.

'Stephen will not be given my name,' he yelled. 'We are not married, and you are a convict so he will have your name and will be on the Stores. Where is the justice in that? I argued that we can't marry because there is no priest here to do the service. Apparently that's not their fault. I decided to take you in as my wife, and you are a convict. So it's my fault.'

If he were a kettle, steam would be coming out of his ears. I'd never seen him this angry and I didn't know what to say. Kitty had told me this might happen, so I wasn't surprised, but it was news to James.

'We'll have his name changed when I finish my sentence, James, or if a priest arrives before then, we can marry and change his name when he is baptised.' I spoke softly, trying to reassure him that it was a problem we could solve in the future.

He bent down and picked up Stephen, snuggling into the baby's neck he whispered that he wanted his son to be a Cullen.

'It's something you are perhaps going to have to get used to, James.' I said while he held our son. 'I am again with child.'

'But so soon?' he said wiping the tears from his face. 'What if you are not ready?'

'Not much can be done about it, James. You're a frisky old man.'

Holding Stephen in one arm he put the other around my shoulders and kissed my cheek.

My tears flowed like a bucket of water being emptied over the potatoes in the garden. I didn't wipe them from my face. Between sobs, I couldn't breathe, and James would hold me until I took a breath. His own blue eyes were red and swollen. He didn't cry in front of me, but I could hear him in the parlour asking God what he'd done to deserve this punishment.

One beautiful summer morning, Stephen didn't wake up. He lay in his little crib next to our bed sleeping with the angels. The surgeon at Sydney Town said there was no explanation, babies just sometimes died no matter how healthy they looked.

Today we bury Stephen next to William at Emily Bay. They'll be together, looking over the blue ocean and flying into the clouds with their angel wings. James promised me again that God would not send our infant to hell because he wasn't baptised. While James lowers the little coffin into the ground I hug my belly and scream out to God to let me keep this child.

15

1799

Cullen held his baby daughter, 'She looks as if she knows everything about the world.' As he spoke, the infant scrunched her eyes and clenched her fists before letting out a scream that prompted him to hand her back to her mother. 'We'll name her Sophia. It means wisdom.'

Settling the infant on to the breast, Elizabeth smiled at Cullen, 'Your daughter is headstrong already, James.'

Leaning in to kiss Elizabeth on the forehead, he stopped himself from saying aloud that he hoped this baby would survive.

Using one of her petticoats, Elizabeth made a baby carrier that went over her shoulders and hung down in front of her. She carried her infant daughter everywhere. Sophia slept between her parents in the large bed her father had made, with her mother waking at the slightest sound or movement.

Cullen understood Elizabeth's obsession with the health and safety of their new infant. His own anxiety at his daughter's wellbeing churned in his stomach every time he left the house.

When she was bundled up safely in his arms he marked off the days she lived, only relaxing a little when she had lived longer than William and Stephen.

'We are moving to my new land purchase as soon as a house is built,' Cullen told Elizabeth as he came into the kitchen for supper. 'The land gives me the opportunity to expand and sell more to the Government Stores as well as trade.'

Bending down to pick up a grizzling Sophia who had been sitting on the floor chewing a crust of bread, Elizabeth said, 'It will need to be a big house, James. Sophia is to have a baby brother or sister. She seems to have survived the curse suffered by our sons, and is thriving. Perhaps our fortunes have changed.'

A grin spreading across his face, James hugged his wife and daughter to him telling them how much he loved them. 'You, Elizabeth, I love more and more each day,' he added.

'It is difficult to believe how my wretched situation in Dublin turned into this wonderful life with you,' she said moving to her favourite chair near the fire to feed her still grizzling daughter.

When supper finished and Sophia settled for the night, Elizabeth joined Cullen in the parlour. He was reading an old newspaper, shaking his head at stories he found disagreeable. Asking him what was going on in the rest of the world, Elizabeth picked up her needlework and sat by the fire opposite her husband.

'There was an uprising in Ireland, they're calling it an Irish Rebellion. The British suppressed it and estimates are between 10,000 and 30,000 deaths.' Cullen watched as Elizabeth gasped and dropped her sewing. 'It's a long way from here, my dear. There may be people you knew who died, but there is nothing we can do. We have a life to keep building on

Norfolk Island. Do you want help writing a letter to your mother?'

Shaking her head, Elizabeth picked up her needlework, trying to see the stitches between her tears.

James Triffitt Jr and his younger brother Thomas crept into Elizabeth's kitchen behind their parents, James and Mary. Sophia squealed her delight and crawled over to the two boys, pulling on Thomas' pants to get his attention.

'You can go and play in the parlour, boys,' Elizabeth told them as she picked up her daughter and led the children into the warm room.

Slicing dried pork and fish for their shared Sunday dinner, Elizabeth commented on how tall Mary's boys were getting.

'I know. They are taller and healthier than any children I remember in London.'

Elizabeth nodded in agreement and told Mary she was with child again.

'That's wonderful news. I am too. We can become huge together.'

While their husbands wandered around James Cullen's farm talking about the weather and plans for the future, Elizabeth and Mary prepared the dinner the two families would share. Triffitt and Cullen had been friends since the early 1790s, Elizabeth slotted into the group when William died. Watching Mary peel boiled eggs, she remembered how frightening the woman seemed when they first met. Yelling at her husband to take off his muddy boots before he went into the house, Mary had turned to Elizabeth still yelling, saying he was her third husband, younger than her, and dumber. She added that they'd flogged her twice since arriving from England, and she didn't know how Triffitt had escaped the same punishment.

The two men sat at either end of the table. James Jr sat near his father on one side and Thomas sat on the other. Mary and Elizabeth were in the middle where they could get up and down when required. Sophia sat in a chair modified by her father, that stopped her from falling onto the floor. She pointed and grunted until they put the chair next to Thomas.

As James Cullen gave thanks for the food and the company, Elizabeth looked around the kitchen at her family and friends. She wiped the tear that trickled down her cheek; thinking about her mother and siblings and the rat-infested cottage in Dublin that they'd shared with two other families.

16

Norfolk Island 1806

In the ten years I've lived on this island, this is the second time I've seen James angrier than a female hog when we take away her babies. They've been talking about making us all move off the island for three or four years; James said they'd forget about it. They haven't. Today they told James we have to pack up and go to Van Diemen's Land at the end of this year. He's sitting in his chair in the parlour. His head is bent over and covered by his hands. I know he's crying. I've never seen him cry. He's wiped tears from his eyes in happiness or sadness, but never fully cried.

Our youngest daughter, Elizabeth—we call her Betsy to save confusion—toddles over to her father and tries to pull his hands away from his face. He doesn't react. I can see his shoulders moving up and down with his sobs. I get Sophia, who is growing fast and is now around eight years, and Catherine seven, to take Betsy outside and keep her occupied.

'James, tell me what I can do.'

'There's nothing we can do. I've begged, cajoled and begged again. The fucking English Government is closing Norfolk Island because it's too hard to get supplies to and from. Doesn't matter that we all have lives here. Triffitt and Morgan and Jones and Hands, and a few others, we went to see John Piper, the Lt Governor. Told him we don't need England, that we can maintain ourselves and our families here without help from the government in London. They won't budge. Very proud to tell us they will pay us double what our land and animals and houses are worth so we can start over in Van Diemen's Land. I'm sixty-five years old, Elizabeth. I don't want to start again. I've been here seventeen years. Why would I want to leave?'

He put his head down again. This time I could hear his crying. I stood next to him and put my arm around his shoulder.

August 1807

The two older girls, Sophia and Catherine know we are leaving our home. Betsy is too little to understand. I've grown tired of trying to explain to them the decision is out of our control and we must leave Norfolk Island. They know no other place.

Coming into the kitchen for dinner, James mumbled that he'd completed the inventory. Trying to diffuse some of the tension, I asked him what he had on his list. 'Sixteen acres in grain and thirty-six in pasture, one male and two female sheep, one male and nine female goats, twenty-eight male and twenty female hogs, and 150 bushels of maize. And the two houses and outbuildings. We leave the day after Christmas on the *Porpoise*.'

I wanted to ask him about our furniture and the animals, but despair hung over him like the rain clouds on the horizon. It could wait.

When the children were asleep I climbed into bed next to

James and cuddled up to him. Before putting his arm around me he wiped his face, not wanting me to see his tears.

'What will happen to the furniture, our other belongings, and the animals?'

'They'll go on a store ship to Van Diemen's Land.'

'The animals too?'

'Some. The remainder will go to the Stores.'

My mind was full of thoughts flapping around like fish just dragged from the water. Sophia and Catherine will want to bring all the animals, especially babies, with us. What will we live in when we get to Van Diemen's Land, and how long will our furniture take to arrive? These were matters best left for now. I wasn't going to risk making James even more sullen with my concerns.

December 1807

Catherine has thrown herself on the floor in the bedroom she shares with Sophia, refusing to pack her clothes and anything else she wants to take to Van Diemen's Land. She's lying face down with her head resting on her arms. Her body is wracking from the sobs. Sophia is sitting on her bed watching her sister, her own tears spilling out of her red eyes like trickles of rain on a window. James is making sure the hogs and the goats are in their yards. They'll be used to feed the people left here on the island, not us. Our new assigned convict Robert Bishop is loading furniture onto a wagon. He and James will drive that into Cascade Bay where it will wait to be loaded onto a ship to follow us to our new home.

I decide to leave Catherine on the floor, and tell Sophia to come into the kitchen to help me pack up enough food to eat on the four day voyage to Hobart Town. I've put in extra just in case. Sophia is as sullen as her father. Of the three girls, she is the one most like him. She has his colouring, his eyes and his demeanour. Catherine is more like me. I'll have to wait till Betsy gets bigger to see who she favours. She sometimes reminds me of my Mammy.

Betsy is asleep on the grass in the shade at the side of the house. Her crib is on the wagon, to be sent on its way with the kitchen table and chairs, our parlour chairs, our mattresses and bedding, our cupboards. James will make us new beds in our new home. We'll be taking our clothes and pots and pans, cups, saucers and plates, and cutlery with us on the *Porpoise*. Some settlers have already left, and others are leaving after us. James and Mary Triffitt are not leaving for another year. I prefer that we are going now. Waiting another year, knowing everything we are doing to improve and look after our farm will be lost, would be too much for James to bear.

James and Robert stride into the kitchen without wiping their feet or taking off their hats. I feel anger rising from my gut to my throat. I'm ready to burst out in a rant over the mess they're making, when I take a deep breath, stopping myself. What's the point? They can make as much mess as they like, we're leaving today, and the English Government will destroy our home.

Patting Sophia on the head, James wants to know where Catherine is. 'She's lying on the floor in our room Papa. She doesn't want to leave.'

'None of us wants to leave. We don't have a choice. I'll get her.'

Catherine follows her father into the kitchen, she's looking at the floor, and her hair is forward covering her face. She's wringing her hands in front of her. My first instinct is to take her to me and hug her, but she will play on that. James has things under control. We must leave.

Betsy is sitting up rubbing her eyes when I go to collect her. The fidgeting and the smell let me know she needs a change. I can't wash the cloth I take off her, so I throw it behind the house. There's enough water in the barrel near the back door to clean her up. Carrying my youngest on my hip, I watch Sophia and Catherine dawdle along behind their father on the way to the cart.

Sophia keeps looking back at the house, wiping her eyes. Catherine's head is down, and she doesn't lift it. James helps me into the back where I sit between bags of clothes and hands me Betsy. Sophia and Catherine climb up on their own and settle where they can. The ten years I've lived on this island rush through my mind. I remember the day I arrived on a cart like this, when James welcomed me and helped me settle. How he looked after me when that Ed raped me, and when baby William died. The grief we shared when we lost Stephen, and the joy when our girls survived infancy. The pride when he got more land and built a grand two-storey home for us, the home I'm now seeing through watery eyes, for the last time. I turn and look at the way ahead, not behind.

10th January 1808

I'm struggling to hide my fear and disappointment from James and the girls. Hobart Town spreads out before us as they help me and the children from the boats, onto the shore. There are scattered houses that look like they belong in the slums of Dublin, a Stores building, a wooden church and a cemetery. I want to turn around swim back to the ship and go home to Norfolk Island.

Looking around for a hotel where we will stay until they tell us where our new land is, I notice the scowl on James' face. His brow is furrowed, and his mouth clenched so tight I wonder if his teeth hurt. Betsy clings to me, hiding behind my skirts while Sophia and Catherine look from the streets of Hobart Town back out to the *Porpoise* and to their father. James stares ahead, his fists are now clenched to match his mouth.

There were around two hundred of us on the *Porpoise*. We are standing in small groups, families and friends, anxious about what is happening next. The scowl on my husband's face is also on the faces of the other men. A person who says he is representing Lt Governor Collins stands at the front of our group, raises his voice and says we will be billeted with families living in Hobart Town. They'll tell us where our land is soon. James calls out to him and wants to know what *soon* means. He ignores the question.

James pulls Robert aside and has a quiet conversation with him before returning to me and the children.

'Robert will stay here with you and the children. I'm going to the Stores. I don't want us billeted with people we don't know. The people we do know, like the Triffitts are still on Norfolk Island. I'll locate two tents – one for Robert and one for us. There's plenty of fresh water and we have the utensils from the kitchen with us. We'll manage for a few days until we know where our land is.'

Sophia and Catherine watch over Betsy while I help James and Robert erect two tents. James found a spot not too far from the water away from the dust kicked up by people traipsing up and down the dirt roads. He and Robert go to the harbour to see where our things are. They make two trips to collect our bedding, cooking utensils, clothes, and the extra food I packed.

Sweat pouring from his brow, James lays down a big sheet of canvas that will be the floor of the tent, and builds a makeshift table out of crates.

'This is home, Elizabeth. I don't know how long we'll be in this dust bowl.'

Standing in the middle of the tent I can feel the sun burning through the top and onto my skin. With nowhere for the heat to go it's like being inside a furnace. Norfolk Island wasn't this hot.

'We should eat outside, James,' I offer. 'At least there's a breeze from the water. It's stifling in here. I'll get something ready for supper then get the girls to bed. It's been a long day.'

17

The Hills, January 1808

James Cullen chose a place out of Hobart Town along the Derwent River where many of the families from Norfolk Island were heading: The Hills. Lt Governor Collins wanted the families moved on as quickly as practicable.

Sailing up the Derwent with his wife and daughters and neighbours from Norfolk Island, Cullen allowed himself a moment to be impressed. The boat sliced through the dark water, hills reflecting either side, and the surrounding vegetation was lush and plentiful. The trees, like the ones he remembered from Port Jackson, towered over the river, offering welcome shade.

Catherine stood up in the boat pointing to the shore, 'Papa, Papa, look at those hens over there.'

Elizabeth pulled her middle daughter back down to her seat, aware of the eyes watching.

'Sit down, child. You can't stand up in small boats like these.'

'But Mama, look at the birds. What are they?'

'They are native hens,' offered the captain of the small vessel. 'They're not often on the riverbank. You are lucky to see them. Keep your eyes out for the Masked Lapwing, they're grey with a funny yellow face. They love the water. There's the Black Currawong too – they make good eating. The Little Pied Cormorant is around these parts as well.'

Straightening her hat and smoothing down her dress, Catherine wanted to know how they were supposed to remember all those strange names.

'You will learn them in time. There's lots of animals and trees here you would never see on Norfolk Island. You'll get used to it.'

Cullen noticed Elizabeth was smiling and pointing out the different birds the captain had mentioned to the children. He hoped that smile would carry them into the unknown future.

After gliding on the river to their new home for what seemed to Cullen like days, the captain announced their destination lay ahead. Taking off his hat and running his fingers through his hair, Cullen's shoulders slumped, and his head dropped. Before them was more of what they had been travelling through along the river.

'What is this all about?' Cullen, the oldest of the settlers demanded of the captain. 'They told us we had land. Where is it? This is the same bush we have been looking at since we left Hobart Town.'

'Don't know,' said the captain while he helped some of the women off the boat. 'There's a few people here from the last lot. They might be able to sort you out. This is called The Hills, and it's where the river becomes freshwater. Good spot. You'll be right. I brought you here. That's my job done.'

The Norfolk Island neighbours stood together on the banks of the river, mothers holding their children close, men off to the side discussing their options. Elizabeth glared at their belongings, unceremoniously dumped on the dirt waiting for collection. She kicked the large cooking pot and watched as the boat turned to make its way back to Hobart Town.

'We'll have to pitch the tents,' James said to Robert Bishop as he ferried Elizabeth and the girls away from the water's edge. 'We'll look for suitable land at first light tomorrow.' Bending to look into Sophia and Catherine's faces, he said to the children, 'Come on girls, help Mama with your things. We're going camping again.'

Elizabeth set up the inside of the tent she and James and the children would call home. Their bedding was on the ground, with a canvas sheet underneath. James made a table from the crates their belongings were packed in, and he'd borrowed two chairs from a settler who'd arrived in the first group. There was no sideboard with a lovely array of china and nowhere to put her pots and pans. The big tub she stored water in, in their beautiful two storey house on Norfolk Island was travelling with their furniture: she and the girls would have to cart water from the river.

Finding enough rocks around the river's edge, Robert built a fireplace between the two tents. The frame from the fireplace in the kitchen on Norfolk Island was with the cooking pot Elizabeth had kicked earlier.

'Thank you, Robert. At least I'll be able to cook whatever you and James find for us to eat.'

James Cullen woke to the sounds of birds he hadn't heard for seventeen years. His back thumped with pain from lying on the ground all night, his hips ached, and his left arm was numb. He rolled off the bedding onto the canvas sheet, careful not to disturb Elizabeth. He'd been lying uncovered all night, in his underwear because it was so hot. The sweat rolled down Elizabeth's forehead into her ear. He marvelled at how she could sleep at all.

Dressed and waiting for him, with the kettle hanging over the fire ready to make tea before the start of their day, Robert Bishop had dragged two fallen trees into the camp area to use as seats.

'Thank you, Robert,' Cullen said smiling at his friend. 'We'll set out to claim our land as soon as we can. Did you hear those birds earlier? Sounded much like the magpies in Port Jackson.'

'I didn't spend any time there, James. Sent straight to Norfolk Island.'

'Lucky you.'

Waking to find James had left, Elizabeth wiped the sweat from her brow and face with her nightdress, and sat up on the bedding. The girls slept. The birds broke the peace of the morning with screeches, squawks, whistles, and throaty sounds never heard on Norfolk Island.

'Hello in there.'

In her own world, worrying about what they were going to do next, Elizabeth jumped in fright. 'Just a moment.'

Pulling her dress over her nightshirt and stuffing her hair under her cap, Elizabeth pulled the door of the tent aside and stepped out into the already scorching heat to greet the person attached to the voice.

'Abraham. How wonderful.'

'I heard you and James arrived yesterday, thought I'd pop down to welcome you to The Hills.' He waved his arm around to show the landscape on the other side of the river. 'I fear I've arrived too early in the day.' His expression reflecting Elizabeth's rushed effort to get dressed.

'I've looked better, on better days. But I've slept in a tent, on the floor, on the hottest night I've ever known.' Elizabeth put her arms around Abraham Hands and gave him a grateful hug. 'It's good to see a friendly face. You make the tea Abraham; the water should be hot. I'll make myself more respectable.'

With her nightshirt removed, Elizabeth's dress sat respectably, and her unruly hair was tamed and tucked neatly under her cap. 'That's better. I'm awake now,' she said to Abraham who waited near the fire.

Sitting on the crates that still contained some of their belongings, Elizabeth poured tea for herself and her guest. 'Tell me what is going on here, Abraham. Tell me what we can expect.'

'Those of us who arrived six months ago and are Class 2 settlers, have dispersed into the bush to stake land claims and build homes. We're struggling to tame the wilderness, to grow food and build homes. Many are still living in tents.' He watched the glint in Elizabeth's eyes turn to a shadow.

'Is James a Class 2 settler?'

'If he's been paid for what he left on Norfolk Island and told he's got land here, then yes.'

As she sat in front of the coals, waving small, relentless flies from her face, and feeling her skin prickle from the already hot sun, Elizabeth plotted revenge against the elements, the wilderness, the river, and the government who sent them here.

18

The Hills

Catherine complains nonstop about little flies buzzing around her face, and Betsy wakes up each morning clawing at the red welts on her arms and legs where mosquitoes feasted on her while she slept. Sophia mopes about the hens she left on Norfolk Island and drags her feet when I ask her to help. It's taken four days for James and Robert Bishop to clear enough land to erect the two tents and set up a permanent camp. James stepped out ten acres within walking distance of the river's edge, and he and Robert pegged out the land claim. He said pegging out the other thirty acres of land was a priority. We'll be living in tents for quite some time.

I haven't looked at myself in a mirror since we got off the *Porpoise* in Hobart Town two weeks ago. My Mammy's voice rings in my ears when I try to put a brush through my hair, 'Ye'll ave rats livin in this mop afore long if ye dono keep it brushed.'

I used to lie in bed at night terrified that the rats I could hear scurrying around the kitchen table and in the walls and roof would take a liking to my hair.

The campsite resembles an ordered life even if it's under canvas instead of a solid roof. James and Robert made a large bed for the girls to share, one for us, and one for Robert for his tent. What furniture we'd sent from Norfolk Island had arrived on the boat from Hobart Town, piled up with everyone else's. The boat's crew unloaded cupboards, tables, chairs, sideboards, cradles, cribs, sofas, stacking them on the riverbank in an order only they seemed to understand. I sent Sophia to find James.

His sunburned face that glowed red in the dark, pulsed purple when he saw the pile of belongings. I noticed his jaw moving as he ground his teeth against each other to contain his rage. His arms hung by his sides; his fists clenched so tight I could see the whites of his knuckles. James hadn't been this wound up since that Ed mongrel raped me all those years ago. I still blame that convict for the death of my William.

Abraham Hands' face was almost as purple as James's, but his body didn't look as if he would pounce on the first thing that moved too close to him. He put his arm around James and led him away from the riverbank. I don't know what he said to him, but James unclenched his fists, took off his hat, wiped his forehead with a kerchief I'd made on Norfolk Island, and put his hat back on his greying hair. The two men walked over to the furniture and between them had the settlers organised into taking what belonged to them. There were no arguments, no fights, no nasty words. It was as if our neighbours were feeling as forlorn as the piles of furniture looked.

With a rare moment to ourselves, James and I take two chairs from the tent and put them next to the outside fire. We don't need the fire to keep warm, but the smoke keeps the mosquitoes away. We need nothing to keep warm. The weather is the most difficult aspect of our new life. The relentless heat continues through the night. When the sun sets, the moon picks up where it left off, making sure the heat, if not the burning of the sun, wears on. I swear if we weren't all so tired from the physicality of our days, none of us would sleep.

James sits close and picks up my hand, folding it in his and raising it to his mouth to kiss. His eyes are drowning in pools of water, the sparkle is left on Norfolk Island.

'I am too old to start again, Elizabeth. But I know I must. I promise to build you a beautiful home here, on this riverbank in New Norfolk. Better than you were forced to leave behind on the island.'

I pull my hand away from him 'Did you say New Norfolk?'

Nodding and smiling and wiping his eyes at the same time, he tells me that the settlers don't like the name *The Hills*, so they've agreed to change it to New Norfolk. Doesn't matter whether the Lt Governor likes it or not, apparently. The decision has been made.

'We are all from Norfolk Island, and this is our new home, it's a fitting name, don't you think?'

Putting my hands around his face and kissing his forehead, I tell him that it's a very fitting name.

April 1808

As much as I hate the hot weather we are forced to endure in New Norfolk, I am pleased we didn't arrive in winter. I've heard stories that it gets so cold it snows. I haven't seen snow since Dublin, and I don't miss it.

'It's too heavy,' Catherine moans when I give her a basket of gardening tools and seedlings to carry.

Taking the basket from her, I pick up Betsy, who is getting heavier by the day, and push her into Catherine's arms. She takes a step backwards and almost drops her younger sister. 'I can't carry her, she's too big.'

Betsy is dumped on the ground on her bottom and kicks Catherine in the shins on her way back to her feet.

Picking up the basket of gardening tools and seedlings, Catherine huffs her way towards the house James is building.

Sophia picks up the shovel, rake and bucket and hurries after her sister before she's given the responsibility of Betsy.

Holding out my hand, Betsy clasps it and we make our way to the house site bearing the food and water we'll need for the day. Looking at the hills surrounding the settlement of New Norfolk, imagining them covered in snow, I tell myself James will finish the house before the weather turns.

May 1808

I overslept, as did the girls. The days are getting shorter, there's a chill in the air, and we were all snug and warm in our own beds, in our own bedrooms. James and Robert finished the house as promised, but the frantic pace has left new furrows and lines on James' face. His brow used to flatten when he wasn't frowning, now it's wrinkled all the time. There are creases around his mouth and his hair is more grey than brown/black.

His side of the bed is empty and cold. He's been gone for a while.

I dress quickly and hurry to the kitchen to see if the fire is going. Of course it is! James would have stoked and thrown more wood on it before he left the house. Looking out the window at a different view, a view of a river instead of rolling pastures that lead to the sea, of trees covered in leaves instead of needles, of multi-coloured parrots trying to get through the netting James put over the new vegetable seedlings, I feel a pang of sadness. The girls will grow up here, instead of paradise.

'Hello, the house,' calls a voice I haven't heard for some time. James and Mary Triffitt and their boys have finally arrived from Norfolk Island.

As if a bugle call woke them, Sophia, Catherine and Betsy run into the kitchen to see who has arrived.

'Go and get dressed, all of you. Visitors don't want to see you in your nightdresses. And brush your hair.' Straightening my own hair, and pulling my sleeves down, I open the kitchen door to greet my friends.

Mary rushes forward and hugs me. Her face against mine is cold, her hands are icy. 'Mary you are freezing, come inside by the fire. You too James, boys, come inside. Where is my husband?'

'He pointed out where we should come, and he and Robert are following with the few belongings we brought with us,' James Triffitt replied.

What ten minutes earlier had been a quiet morning with birds making all the noise, is now filled with children competing to be heard and adults talking at the same time.

As Mary Triffitt warmed up, she peeled off her jacket and scarf. 'Is it always this cold, here?'

'We haven't been here for a winter yet, but people in Hobart Town said it gets cold enough to snow.' She moved sideways while I put more wood on the fire.

'James Triffitt will just have to find us somewhere to live then. I'm not living in a tent in this weather.'

'You'll stay with us until you're settled, Mary. I wouldn't have our Norfolk Island friends perishing in a tent if I can help it,' James said as he and Robert brought the Triffitt's belongings into the kitchen. 'We've got two outbuildings, Robert is well set up in one of them, the boys could bunk in with him, James you and Mary can have our girls' room, and they can sleep in the parlour. We'll work it out. You can store the things you're not using in the stable.'

Sophia, Catherine, James Jr and Thomas clapped hands, clearly delighted at the decisions my husband made. I wasn't so sure. But we had little choice than to offer accommodation to our friends.

James Triffitt and his eldest son left the house at dawn prepared to find choice land in what was being called *Back River*. Mary started the day grumbling about how cold it was, and how she wished our husbands had made more of a fuss about leaving Norfolk Island. I didn't comment on the weather or her protest.

'Sit down, Mary. There's a fresh pot of tea and oats from our rations. I'll get the children.'

Thomas, Sophia, Catherine and Betsy were easier to manage than Mary Triffitt. She sat sulking at the kitchen table, still in her nightdress, her overcoat pulled in tight around her. With her hands clasped around the mug of tea I poured earlier she showed no interest in getting the children organised for the day. Sophia stirred the oatmeal in the pot over the fire, adding more water so it would go further, and Catherine showed Thomas where he could wash his face and comb his hair. Betsy followed him, asking if he needed any help, delighting in the company of someone other than her sisters.

I left Mary in the kitchen, made sure the children were rugged up against the cold and set off to get some work done. As soon as he spotted James, Thomas ran off to help with the hen house. The girls and I worked on the vegetable plot, getting the soil ready for winter planting. We needed to be self-sufficient sooner rather than later. Robert travelled into Hobart Town on the river every week to get our rations, and as varied as they could be for the number of people living on the Stores, we needed our own food.

Still with her overcoat wrapped around her, Mary came to the garden which James had established on the northern side of the house. At least she was dressed, even though her hair hung around her shoulders like a crow's nest. After asking me what I was planting, she scoffed at my response.

'How do you know peas, carrots and cabbage will grow? It's so damned cold here, I think we'll all starve to death before summer.'

Sophia and Catherine watched me put down the trowel and stand up. They stayed kneeling on the dirt, their heads tilted so as not to miss my retort.

'Reverend Knopwood has grown these vegetables success-fully for four years, Mary,' I said ever so sweetly. 'He gave James the seedlings. So, with his blessings, and my hard work, of course they'll grow.'

Not waiting for a response from my disgruntled, bad tempered house guest, I knelt back on the soil and kept digging.

James Triffitt and his sons cleared enough land to erect a small cabin for the family. Four weeks after they sailed up the Derwent River into our lives, and just as the real winter set in, Mary packed up her family's belongings and James and I helped her load them onto a wagon her husband had bought in Hobart Town. Her eldest son, James Jr took the reins and flicked them on the back of the bullock. I stood with an arm linked in my husband's and waved goodbye with the other. Our girls ran after the wagon, waving and calling that they would see the boys soon.

'Not too soon,' I promised myself.

19

Winter 1809

With the girls getting older and able to help more, Elizabeth had established a thriving vegetable garden. Many of the Norfolk Island settlers were still on Government Stores. James would not hear of his family subsisting on handouts from the Government. With Robert Bishop, who stayed on as a farm hand after his sentence expired, Cullen had sheep, pigs and hens. They had enough to eat without having to hunt the native wildlife. Those Norfolk Island neighbours who bemoaned their lot in Van Diemen's Land and sat back waiting for the promised Government compensation for the property they left behind, were still living in tents, still waiting. Cullen, Triffitt, Hands, Roger Gavin and some others, cleared their land and built houses before the Government had caught up with the titles. There was no need to wait.

The rain pelted on the window shutters, drops seeping in between the slats. Elizabeth put towels she couldn't spare over the shutters, on the inside, to stop the water coming into the house. It was a battle she wasn't winning. The towels became sodden and in need of replacement quicker than the wet ones were drying.

'Is it ever going to stop, James? The vegetables will wash away.'

'I know. It's the river I'm concerned about. The level is rising by the hour.'

Donning his waterproof coat, boots and hat, Cullen opened the front door of his house and stepped out on to the verandah. Sloshing his way through the mud he made his way to the stable where Robert Bishop and James' friend, Roger Gavin were preparing the animals for a prolonged stay inside.

'The billy goat doesn't want to be restrained,' Robert told him. 'He's put up a hell of a struggle.'

Looking at the state of his friends, their clothes having lost all their shape and their faces and hands blue from the cold, Cullen felt a wave of gratitude wash over him.

'Thank you, both. I wouldn't be able to manage without you two.'

Ignoring the complement, Robert rounded up the nanny goats and kids and put them in a pen, with not much more than standing room.

Roger herded the sheep into an enclosure they'd put up at the back of the stable. The horse shared another fenced off section with two cows. 'It's not going to smell too good in here if the rain keeps up for much longer.'

Standing in the stable's doorway wiping the rain from his face, and looking toward the Derwent, James shook his head from side to side. 'We will protect the stable and the house from floodwaters if the river keeps rising.'

With no sand to fill wheat sacks, Robert Bishop suggested using dirt. 'It's mud now, but the three of us should get enough bags filled before it's too late.'

Thankful he'd collected wheat sacks from the Stores on his last few visits to Hobart Town, Cullen, Robert and Roger each collected a shovel, a handful of sacks and headed to the house.

The drudgery of placing sacks around the foundations of the house and filling them with mud saw the three men collapse on the verandah after they filled the last bag.

'Triffitt had the right idea staking out land up on the Back River, away from the Derwent,' Cullen said as he shook the water from his hat.

Wringing the water out of his own hat, Robert said the small river that ran through Triffitt's property would probably flood with all this rain too.

Roger Gavin whose land was further from the river than Cullen's, agreed. 'I'm grateful I haven't planted vegetables yet. Looking at yours James, I think your family might be on the Stores a lot longer when this rain stops.'

Shaking his head to disagree, Cullen explained how Elizabeth had preserved, bottled and dried the summer vegetables and fruits. 'We'll be fine as long as we keep the animals from drowning.'

At the mention of the animals, Cullen put his sopping wet hat back on his head, struggled to his feet, picked up a shovel, and made his way to the stable.

Roger waved goodbye, Cullen's gratitude wringing in his ears as he made his way on the once firm but now boggy track to his land grant.

With all the wheat sacks taken up to protect the house, Cullen and Robert Bishop used the shovels to dig a trench around the permitter of the stable. Mud was slapped against the foundations and part way up the walls outside to keep out any rising water.

Not bothering to take their sodden hats off, the men sloshed through the mud and the pelting rain back to the house. Opening the door slightly, James called to Elizabeth.

'Please bring a blanket for Robert and one for me. We'll have to strip our clothes out here.'

Blankets held in tight against their frozen bodies, Cullen and Robert Bishop huddled in front of the fire. Cullen's teeth chattered and his body shook. Catherine gave her father and his friend a pair of socks to cover their blue toes.

'Oh, Papa, you must warm up. She took one of the last dry towels from Elizabeth and gave it to her father to dry his hair. 'You'll have to share with Mr Bishop. That's all we have left.'

'All the animals survived. The water didn't get in under the floor or the footings, but the roof leaked some,' Robert reported after the rain eased and glimpses of sunshine could be seen through the retreating clouds. 'Can't say the same for your garden, Elizabeth.'

Shrugging her shoulders, Elizabeth put more wood on the fire, and prepared a mug of tea to take to her husband, adding a dash of rum. Lying on the settee in the parlour, Cullen used a towel to wipe sweat from his face.

'Move away from the fire, James. You are too hot.'

'If I do I get cold and shiver.'

'Then find a place halfway.' Moving a rocking chair into the centre of the room, Elizabeth helped her husband from the settee into the chair. 'When you're cold, cover up. When you're hot, remove blankets. Drink this tea.'

Elizabeth left Sophia to watch over James, ushering the other two girls into the kitchen. Robert had slaughtered two of the weaker hens and their white flesh was now simmering in a pot over the fire. With carrots and onions salvaged before the rain flooded the vegetable garden, Elizabeth taught Catherine and Betsy how to make chicken soup.

Creeping into bed next to her husband, Elizabeth felt the

heat from his body spreading across the sheets. 'Push the blankets off, James, you are hot.'

'I am not feeling any better. I feel like I'm going to die.'

'You will not die. I won't stand for it. You've got a chill from working in the rain and the mud. Rest and you'll recover.'

'If I recover, my dear, we will be married. It is an event that is long overdue.'

25th September 1809

With the promise of fine weather lingering over New Norfolk, Mary Triffitt helped Elizabeth with her hair, and showed Sophia and Catherine how to tie a decorative bow at the back of their mother's new dress.

'Two goats sold to the Stores,' Elizabeth said when she looked in the mirror at the new dress James had ordered from Sydney.

'It'll be a long time before you get another one, I'd wager,' Mary said while she put Elizabeth's cap on her brushed, wavy, black hair.

Knocking on the parlour door, Cullen waited for an invitation to enter the room.

'You look lovely, my dear.'

His kiss quickened Elizabeth's heart. Even though they'd lived as husband and wife for over ten years, today she would become Mrs James Bryan Cullen. 'I love you, James.'

'And I you. Since the day I first saw you, struggling down off the cart, shaking like the leaves on an oak tree when a storm takes hold.'

'Alright, enough of that. Time to get to the river. Reverend Knopwood doesn't strike me as a patient man.' Mary Triffitt ushered Elizabeth, Sophia, Catherine and Betsy out of the house toward the river and the jetty James had built.

Waving them off, Mary and James Triffitt watched until the family was out of sight around the bend.

Elizabeth sat on the bench that ran along the perimeter of the little boat, watching James as his body moved to a rhythm only he could hear. His strong arms moved the oars in the water, while his upper body swayed back and forth keeping in time with the oars.

Along with his friends Roger Gavin and Robert Bishop, James had established a rotation so that while one man rested, the other two rowed. They would arrive at St David's Church in Hobart in plenty of time. They wouldn't test Reverend Knopwood's patience today.

After he'd helped Elizabeth and his daughters from the boat, James Cullen took off his hat, swept it in front of him and bowed. 'Let us make our way to church so we can be married.'

'Come in, come in,' Reverend Robert Knopwood held the door while James, Elizabeth and the girls made their way into the small church. James' friend Roger Gavin was in place at the side of the altar, and another man Elizabeth didn't know, stood on the other side. Robert Bishop sat in one of the pews.

'Why is Robert not standing with Roger? Who is that man with him?' Elizabeth fretted as she walked beside James to the altar.

'Robert can't be a witness my dear. He has not learned to read and write. He can't sign his name. William Stokes will do so in his place.'

'I can't read and write either. How am I to sign the certificate?'

'You will put your mark, Elizabeth. Robert Knopwood will write your name next to it. A witness must be literate. Let's not be worried about it. Let's just get married.'

When James finished promising Elizabeth he would love

her until death took him, he placed a gold band on the third finger of her left hand. She held it up to the light, moving her wrist so the ring sparkled in the morning sunshine. 'Can we afford this?' she whispered as James lent in to kiss her. A wink and a cheeky smile were her answer.

20

Address

From the inhabitants of New Norfolk [1]

To his Excellency Lachlan Macquarie, Esq.
Captain General and Governor in Chief in and over
His Majesty's Territory of New South Wales and its Dependencies.

The inhabitants of New Norfolk, a settlement formed under the jurisdiction of Hobart Town, most dutifully presume to return Your Excellency our most sincere thanks for your condescension in visiting our Settlement.

Our industrious exertions are fully compensated on receiving your Excellency's approbation, and we pledge ourselves in future to persevere to the utmost in honest industry, and every effort to advance by agriculture, to the interest of the Colony in

general, to merit a continuance of your Excellency's generous
and kind patronage.

Our gratitude for allowing us to remain on the King's stores
shall never be effaced from our memories, and our children
shall be instructed as soon as their articulation commence to
list the name of Governor Macquarie, and dutifully in behalf of
their brother settlers subscribe ourselves

Your Excellency's most grateful servants
"Signed" D. McCarty
J. Triffith (sic)
J.B Cullen
A. Hands

His Excellency's Answer

2

Hobart Town, Van Diemen's Land
Saturday November 30th 1811
To MessrsDennis McCarty
James B Cullen
James Triffith (sic) and
Abraham Hands

You will be so good as to acquaint the inhabitants of the
District of New Norfolk, that the Address you have this day
presented to me, from them has proved highly gratifying to me,
and that I receive as a Pledge of their resolution to persevere in
that course of honest industry, so happily begun – the benefi-
cial result of which is the pleasant pleasing prospect of their

enjoying the fruits of their labour in an abundant harvest, I have so recently witnessed in my inspection of the District. I beg you will assure the settlers and other inhabitants of New Norfolk that I shall ever take a lively interest in their welfare and prosperity and that it will always afford me sincere pleasure to extend every reasonable indulgence to such of them as prove themselves worthy of it, by persevering in habits of honest industry, sobriety and morality.

I am, etc.
"Signed" L. Macquarie

11th November 1811

'Hold still, James. Let me brush the jacket. I don't want you walking out of here with bits of wheat husk sticking out in odd directions. And when we're done, don't go outside. Sit in the parlour and wait for James Triffitt.' Elizabeth's pride at her husband being one of four New Norfolk settlers chosen to greet Governor Macquarie on his historic visit to the Derwent Valley, spread across her face when she turned him around to look at her. 'You are a real gentleman, James. Handsome. You are a landowner, a settler and a respected member of this community. I'm proud of you.'

'I'm nervous about speaking to Governor Macquarie. Although the four of us have spent days working on our welcome, I still worry it isn't perfect.'

'Of course it is perfect, James.'

'Hello, the house,' James Triffitt called as he pushed open the front door to James and Elizabeth's home. 'Let's go, my friend. We will meet Abraham at Denis McCarty's place.

Making sure her daughters had their hats, had washed their faces and brushed their hair, Elizabeth followed her husband

and Triffitt to the boat where Mary Triffitt and her sons James and Thomas waited.

'This is the most exciting day since we were dumped here,' Mary chirped. 'Imagine meeting Governor Macquarie. He's bringing his wife, too. Shame that McCarty's place was chosen for the event. Yours is much nicer, Elizabeth.'

'Thank you, Mary. Thanks to James and Robert we do have a nice house. But Denis McCarty is one of the original settlers at New Norfolk, and a Constable. The honour must go to him.'

Travelling the short distance to McCarty's farm on the river in the warm November sun calmed Mary Triffitt's temper.

The breeze created as the oars skimmed through the surface of the Derwent ruffled James' hair. The hair Elizabeth had spent at least ten minutes trying to tame. 'Put your hat on, James,' she called to him over the heads of the children.

Turning to offer her a scowl, James left his hat on the seat next to him, and kept reading over the speech he was giving on behalf of the community.

Coming from McCarty's house, Abraham Hands offered to help Elizabeth and Mary. Elizabeth took his arm and stepped onto the little jetty McCarty had built for the Governor's boat.

Mary Triffitt insisted she could manage on her own. Her husband stood by, his hand over his mouth to hide a smirk. Mary tripped but regained her footing before she fell. Face as red as the trim on her dress, Mary lifted her head and stomped off towards the other waiting guests.

'The whole of New Norfolk is here, James.' Elizabeth smiled at people she knew while they walked the gauntlet of onlookers to the verandah of Dennis McCarty's house.

Shaking Cullen's hand and pecking Elizabeth on the cheek, McCarty offered them a seat. Abraham Hands sat next to Cullen, and James and Mary Triffitt the other side. McCarty's fiancée Marianne sauntered up and down waiting for her esteemed guests to arrive.

Just after two thirty, they heard the call, 'The boat's just past the Government Farm.'

Cullen, Triffitt, Hands and McCarty made their way to the edge of the river, leaving their wives, children and soon to be wife, waiting at the house. When Governor Macquarie's boat came into view, Cullen's stomach lurched into his throat. He needed very deep breaths to stop his breakfast from spilling out on to his second-hand suit.

'Your Excellency, Mrs Macquarie,' Dennis McCarty bowed to his guests, 'welcome to New Norfolk.'

Putting his hand forward to shake McCarty's, Governor Macquarie was introduced to Cullen, Hands and Triffitt. 'I am most pleased to meet you all.'

Cullen wiped his hand on his pants to clean off the sweat that had gathered there while he watched the Governor and Mrs Macquarie step out of the boat. Shaking Lachlan Macquarie's hand, Cullen nodded and said they were honoured to meet him.

'I am charged with the official welcome, Your Excellency.' Clearing his throat, Cullen launched into the address the four friends had prepared. Macquarie listened.

'Thank you, gentlemen, and Mr Cullen for your learned execution of the Address. I will respond before I return to Sydney.'

Pushing Cullen aside Denis McCarty put his hand behind Macquarie's back and led him to the house for afternoon tea.

Elizabeth Cullen sat next to Elizabeth Macquarie while the men fawned over the Governor. The children, ordered outside by McCarty's fiancée, put their faces to the windows to get a better look at the special visitors.

'It is very gracious of you and the Governor to visit us, Mrs Macquarie,' Elizabeth said as she passed a plate of lemon slice.

'I must admit we are both quite surprised by the industrious situation we find most of you in. Your farms are a testament to the hard work and dedication of settlers from Norfolk Island.'

'Yes. My poor husband is sixty-nine years old. It's been a huge effort to build a new life here when the one we had on Norfolk Island was plentiful and peaceful.'

Mrs Macquarie patted Elizabeth's hand 'I can't imagine. Mrs McCarty, is there any more tea?'

Taking leave of her place at the table, Elizabeth made her way through the throngs of people crowded at the front of Dennis McCarty's house. Sophia, Catherine and Betsy sat under a tree with Thomas Triffitt. The children were laughing.

'Where's your Mama, Thomas?'

Standing as soon as Elizabeth spoke, Thomas pointed to a crowd gathered at the side of the house. 'Mama is trying to talk to Governor Macquarie.'

Mary Triffitt stood behind the Governor's entourage, craning her neck to get a look at His Excellency. A short woman, she found it impossible to see over the heads of the men in front. Elizabeth watched as Mary bent at the waist to peer through the gaps between the onlookers. The children giggled as Mary gave up and went into the house.

With the Governor and his wife ensconced at Dennis McCarty's for the night, the Norfolk Island settlers returned to their farms.

James Cullen climbed into bed without changing into his nightshirt. Lying on his back waiting for Elizabeth he went through the day's activities over and over, wondering if Lachlan Macquarie was really as pleased with the development of New Norfolk as he indicated.

'Why are you lying there with nothing on, James?'

'I'm too tired to be bothered. I keep thinking about the day and hope that Macquarie's praise was genuine.'

Elizabeth cuddled in close to her husband, 'Of course it was genuine. Those of us who have tried have done a marvellous job taming the land and becoming self-sufficient. Your Address was brilliant of course.'

'He said he is going to name the settlement Elizabeth Town after his wife. I can't see that sticking. It's been New Norfolk since 1807 and we will be making sure that's how it stays.' James pulled his wife into him, kissing her and saying that if it was Elizabeth Town it would be after her, not Mrs Macquarie.

21

October 1812

'Why are you going to Hobart Town, Papa?' Sophia had been hinting to her father about a new dress; exaggerating how she needed more than two dresses because she was growing taller every day.

'I'm not getting a dress this trip, Sophia. Mama will make you a new dress when the fabric arrives from London. You'll have to squeeze into the ones you have, a bit longer. This time I'm bringing back a convict assignee to help around the farm.'

'We don't want a convict on the farm, Papa,' Betsy said helping Cullen put his things into the boat as it bobbed up and down on the river.

Cullen's brow furrowed and the smile that always accompanied conversations with his daughters, disappeared. 'What are you saying, child?'

'Sophia said convicts steal things and tell lies. The convicts on Mr Triffitt's farm are liars and thieves.'

Taking Betsy's hand, Cullen guided her from the boat and told her to sit down on the riverbank with him. 'Some convicts are bad people. Some who are not convicts are bad. People are people. Being a convict doesn't make you a bad person.'

Looking up into her father's weather beaten face, Betsy asked how he knew.

'Get your sisters and meet me in the kitchen and I'll tell you.'

Sitting on one side of the table next to Elizabeth, Cullen told the three girls to sit opposite. 'Seems Betsy has decided she doesn't want a convict assignee working on the farm. And Sophia believes all convicts to be thieves and liars. What do you think, Catherine?'

Shaking her head, the middle daughter said she didn't know what to think.

'Mama and I were convicts.' He let the statement sink in, watching each girls' reaction. Catherine shrugged her shoulders, not seeming to care, Sophia slapped her hand to her mouth and Betsy's eyes bulged to the point Cullen thought they'd pop out of her head.

'Mr Triffitt was a convict. Mr Hands and Mr McCarty were convicts. Robert Bishop was a convict. My friend, Roger Gavin was a convict. Mrs Triffitt was a convict. Do you want me to go on?'

'But that can't be so,' Betsy protested. 'Mr McCarty is the Constable.'

'That's right,' Elizabeth said to her daughter. 'It doesn't matter what he was in the past, he is now the Constable. All of the adults in New Norfolk were once convicts, Papa and I included.'

'But you are not liars and thieves,' Betsy protested. 'Sophia said convicts were liars and thieves.'

'No I didn't,' the eldest child screamed. 'Thomas Triffitt said that.'

'It doesn't matter who said what,' Cullen growled. 'You can't judge people by what someone else says. Do you understand?'

The three girls nodded.

'So when I bring home a new worker you will be respectful and polite as per your upbringing. You will not ask him questions about why he is a convict. Now I have to go.'

Kissing his wife, Cullen told her he would be back in a couple of days.

'Have you thought about how other people see us, Robert?' Cullen asked his friend as New Norfolk disappeared around the bend.

'There are some so called free settlers in Hobart Town that look down their noses at the likes of us, James. But we've got the upper hand. We've been here longer and know what's what. It's not something that bothers me.'

'You don't yet have any children, Robert.'

The trip up the Derwent River was uneventful, giving Cullen time to reflect on his daughters' assumptions about men and women serving a sentence in Van Diemen's Land. Neither he nor Elizabeth had considered telling the children about their convict past. It hadn't seemed relevant to their current situation. He wondered how many other children of convicts had opinions that didn't marry with their reality.

'Leave the goods to me to take to the Stores, James. You'll be occupied enough taking charge of a new convict.' Robert Bishop winked at his friend and watched as he made his way to the Superintendent's office. The Stores sent a cart to meet the boat and Robert loaded the wheat and maize from Cullen's farm onto the back.

The money from the sale of the farm produce would go towards building the house Cullen had promised Elizabeth since they lived as husband and wife on Norfolk Island.

'What's the new convict list like?' Robert asked Mr

Williams, the manager of the Stores while he stacked the wheat sacks in the designated area.

'The usual I'd say. Some will be trouble and finish their sentences and then some. Others are like you, Robert: something minor sees a major upheaval. James Cullen will make sure he gets a good worker.'

Robert watched the man being pushed towards the frame in the centre of the yard. A guard, rotten teeth showing as he grinned at the onlookers, moved his arm back and let fly with a mighty grunt as the whip pierced the flesh on the back of the poor sod tied by his wrists to the top of the wooden structure. Forcing the bile that lurched from his stomach into his throat back down, Robert Bishop saw the horror on the faces of the convicts bearing witness to the punishment. They weren't there willingly.

Cullen stood on the other side of the circle watching as the guard poised to make his first strike. When the victim screamed in agony, the scars on Cullen's back prickled. *This shouldn't still be happening.*

Moving away from the crowd, shaking his head in disgust as much as pity for the poor man tied to the frame, Cullen continued to the Superintendent's Office.

'Come in, Mr Cullen, sit down. May I offer you a refreshment?'

'No thank you, Superintendent, just want to collect the convict and make my way home.'

'Well, you'll have to wait a day or so I'm afraid Mr Cullen. The one we assigned to you is just being untied from the frame in the middle of the yard.'

To be continued in Book 1 – NO ROOM FOR REGRET

ALSO BY JANEEN ANN O'CONNELL

The story continues in Book One of the Cullen/Bartlett Dynasty:

NO ROOM FOR REGRET published by Next Chapter, and available in eBook on Amazon.

It continues in Book Two LOVE, LIES, AND LEGACIES published by NextChapter.pub

And

Book Three TIME TELLS ALL published by Next Chapter

VISIT : janeenannoconnell.com for up to date information.

And my Facebook page

Janeen Ann O'Connell Author

Please be kind enough to review the book on Amazon.com, or

Amazon.com.au, or Goodreads.

Thank you.

janeeno@outlook.com

Dear reader,

We hope you enjoyed reading *The Conviction of Hope*. Please take a moment to leave a review, even if it's a short one. Your opinion is important to us.

Discover more books by Janeen Ann O'Connell at https://www.nextchapter.pub/authors/janeen-ann-oconnell

Want to know when one of our books is free or discounted? Join the newsletter at http://eepurl.com/bqqB3H

Best regards,

Janeen Ann O'Connell and the Next Chapter Team

You might also like:
No Room for Regret by Janeen Ann O'Connell

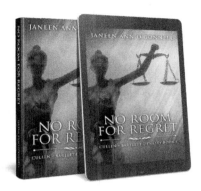

To read the first chapter for free, please head to:
https://www.nextchapter.pub/books/no-room-for-regret

ABOUT THE AUTHOR

Retired secondary teacher, Janeen Ann O'Connell has been researching the murky convict past of her family tree for many years. The convict stain was secreted away by well-meaning descendants.

Janeen's perseverance and excellent research skills gave voice to the long buried and long forgotten souls who were transported to the other side of the world as a form of punishment for minor crimes. In recognising them, she gives them permission to tell their stories in the books of the Cullen/Bartlett dynasty.

NOTES

Chapter 1

1. Transcribed from: *Proceedings of the Old Bailey, 6th April 1785, page 60.*

Chapter 2

1. The First Fleet by Rob Mundle. Harper Collins Australia (2015) p. 68

Chapter 3

1. The First Fleet. Rob Mundle. Harper Collins, Australia, 2015. Pg 71-72
2. The First Fleet by Rob Mundle. Harper Collins Australia, 2015 p. 91
3. The First Fleet, by Rob Mundle. Harper Collins (Australia) 2015, p.129
4. The First Fleet by Rob Mundle. Harper Collins (Australia) 2015 p. 134

Chapter 4

1. The First Fleet, by Rob Mundle. Harper Collins (Australia) 2015. P.164
2. www.australianfoodtimeline.com.au/first-colonists-food/

Chapter 5

1. www.convictcreations.com/history/punishments.html
2. The Founders of Australia: a Biographical Dictionary of the First Fleet by Mollie Gillen. Sydney: Library of Australian History, 1989

Chapter 6

1. https://www.navyhistory.org.au/hms-sirius-australias-first-flagship
2. www.monumentaustralia.org.au/themes/disaster/maritime/display/22588-h.m.s.-sirius

Chapter 20

1. Colonial Secretary's Papers – New South Wales State Archives. (Special Bundles 1794-1825)
2. Colonial Secretary's Papers – New South Wales State Archives. (Special Bundles 1794-1825)

Printed in Great Britain
by Amazon